SILKE'S QUEST

A SILKE JUSTICE NOVEL #2
by

KEN FARMER

Cover Art

K. R. Farmer
Adriana Girolami

AUTHOR

Ken Farmer didn't write his first full novel until he was sixty-nine years of age. He often wonders what the hell took him so long. At age seventy-eight...he's currently working on novel number thirty-one.

Ken spent thirty years raising cattle and quarter horses in Texas and forty-five years as a professional actor (after a stint in the Marine Corps). Those years gave him a background for storytelling...or as he has been known to say, "I've always been a bit of a bull---t artist, so writing novels kind of came naturally once it occurred to me I could put my stories down on paper."

Ken's writing style has been likened to a combination of Louis L'Amour and Terry C. Johnston with an occasional Hitchcockian twist...now that's a combination.

In addition to his love for writing fiction, he likes to teach acting, voice-over and writing workshops. His favorite expression is: "Just tell the damn story."

Writing has become Ken's second life: he has been a Marine, played collegiate football, been a Texas wildcatter, cattle and horse rancher, professional film and TV actor and director, and now...a novelist. Who knew?

Ken Farmer's dialogue flows like a beautiful western river...it's the gold standard...Carole Beers

Web page: www.KenFarmer-Author.net

ISBN-13: 978-1-7329119-9-4
ISBN-10: 1-7329119-9-1

Timber Creek Press
Imprint of Timber Creek Productions, LLC
312 N. Commerce St.
Gainesville, Texas 76240

Published by: Timber Creek Press
timbercreekpresss@yahoo.com
www.timbercreekpress.net
Twitter: @pagact
Facebook Book Page:
www.facebook.com/TimberCreekPress
Ken's email: pagact@yahoo.com
214-533-4964

ACKNOWLEDGMENT

The author gratefully acknowledges Lt. Colonel
Clyde DeLoach, USMC (Ret.), Buck Stienke, Terry
D. Heflin - retired English Professor at Tarrant
County College, and award-winning, best-selling
novelist Mary Deal, for their invaluable help in
proofing, beta reading and editing this novel.

FOREWARD
by
MARY DEAL

Silke's Quest is a sequel to Ken Farmer's wonderful new best seller, *Silke Justice*, the top lady Pinkerton detective. It includes new characters along with the familiar, Bone and Loraine, Padrino, and Texas Ranger Riley Boston.

Silke—and her half wolf, Bear Dog—Bone, Loraine, and Padrino follow the mastermind of the KATY railroad robberies into the eerie primordial Caddo Lake—225,000 acres of cypress swamp with a 25 to 30 thousand acre lake in the middle. He also has Elizabeth, his nine year old niece with him.

They rescue a group of teens on vacation under siege by a clan of inbred cannibalistic moonshiners with the help of the father of one of the teens, Marshal Farmer from Gainesville. They are also assisted by a mysterious teen, Maggie, the daughter of the mastermind's twin brother, James.

Silke's Quest is chock full of action, suspense, pathos, and a bit of the unknown with characters you'll love and characters you'll love to hate. I have to say…it's a trip you won't want to miss. The ending is another one of the type this author is famous for. It creeps up from nowhere and leaves you gasping. You won't see it coming.

TIMBER CREEK PRESS

CHAPTER ONE

DENISON, TEXAS

"Forgot my rifle, honey," Timothy McPherson looked down at his nine year old niece, Elizabeth, as he set her on the sidewalk.

She held Sally, her rag doll, tightly to her thin chest as she looked up at him.

The tall man with the silver temples took her hand, they turned around, and headed back toward his sister's small white clapboard house.

They were only a block away when McPherson abruptly stopped in the shadow of a large tree. He could see the Pinkerton Detective, Silke Justice, man-mountain Deputy Sheriff Darrell Bone, and his wife, Deputy Sheriff Loraine Bone, exit the front door of house and stand on the porch in the pale moonlight.

He knew they undoubtedly had found his sister and Elizabeth's mother, Sarah Haas' body where he left her on the kitchen floor in a puddle of blood—her own butcher knife embedded in her chest. They would never believe it was an accident.

"Look, Unka Mack, that's the Pinkerton lady that gave us that money…She's really nice…Oh, and Bear Dog's with her." Elizabeth looked up at her uncle with her big blue eyes. "I like her…and her puppy."

The pretty blonde-haired child tugged on his hand, trying to pull him on toward the house.

He held back. "Uh…no, honey, we don't have time to go back."

"What about your rifle?"

"I'll...I'll get another, come on."

They turned around, he picked her up again and with long strides, headed toward downtown Denison.

"Apparently, not only was McPherson our sniper...No question this is the same rifle he carried when he visited our camp..." said Silke, holding up the Mauser rifle he left in his sister's house. "...but, it looks like he was also the mastermind behind the railroad robberies...with help from her."

Bear Dog's head snapped to the right as his blue eyes stared down the street and whined.

"What is it, boy?" Silke followed his gaze down the shadowy street. "There's nothin' down there."

"Glad we had our crime scene kit in our saddlebags," commented Bone. "I'm sure the prints on the knife and the rifle will match." He held up his smart phone he used to take close-up pictures of the print adhesive tape they had used.

"Not to say anything about murdering his sister and kidnapping Elizabeth," said Loraine. "We know he was here."

Silke shook her head and tightened her lips. "Glad ya'll had your kits...Lizbeth is such a sweet baby." She looked at Bone and Loraine. "With God as my witness...I will find him...and it won't be pretty. He can run, but he can't hide."

"He's the worst kind of scum," said Bone. "Pretending to be a respectable businessman and owner of the Painted Lady Saloon...Wonder what kind of a trail he left behind him before he came to Gainesville?"

"Leopards don't change their spots," commented Silke...

SANTA FE DEPOT
GAINESVILLE, TEXAS

It was well after 10 PM when the west bound train rolled to a stop at the depot, blowing steam from her relief valves on both sides of the boiler.

Bone looked out the side window of the car at the red brick platform next to the depot building, dimly lit by two gas lamps. "Doc Wellman's here...So's Padrino."

They got to their feet, Bone and Bodie each took an end of the litter and followed Silke, Loraine, and Bear Dog to the exit at the front of the car.

Wellman immediately checked Riley's pulse and his eyes when they stepped down the steps and nodded. "Just like Doctor Ashalatubbi told me in his telegram…eyes dialated, he's cuncussed, but his pulse is strong…My buckboard is out front, boys. Got a bunch of quilts in the back."

"Want us to follow you?" asked Padrino.

"You don't mind…I'll need help getting him inside. My nurse has already gone home. Lucy said she would be at my clinic in the morning."

"His eyes have fluttered a few times, Doc," said Silke. "Think he's tryin' to wake up?"

The tall sixty year old physician shook his head. "Not necessarily, Miss Justice, he could have some spasms also…I'm hoping that there's only epidural hemorrhage."

"What's that?" she asked.

"Bleeding inside the skull, but outside the dura…or the covering of the brain. It's sort of like the fascia under the hide of a deer…"

"If it's something more?"

"Well, if it's *subdural* hemorrhage…inside the covering, and possibly in the brain itself…He could have permanent brain damage too…never waking up…Only time will tell."

Silke nodded somberly. "Got it."

Bone and Bodie carefully laid the litter on the quilts Doctor Wellman had layered in the bed of the buckboard. Silke crawled up into the back and sat beside the injured ranger. She reached over and took one of his hands and held it tightly.

"Go with Loraine, Bear Dog." Silke pointed at the black carriage behind them.

"Be right behind you, Doc," said Padrino as he stepped up into the driver's seat of Faye's Phaeton and picked up the reins.

Bone, Loraine, and Bodie followed him and sat in the back. Bear Dog laid down on the floorboard, his head between his paws.

Padrino cherked to the matched set of sorrel standardbred geldings and pulled in behind Doctor Wellman's buckboard as they headed across California Street to Dixon, and then to Main Street headed west.

BAKER HOTEL
DENISON, TEXAS

"Did mama hurt herself bad, Unka Mack?" asked Lizbeth as she crawled up on one of the beds in their room and sat up, looking at her uncle.

McPherson paused for a moment, and then nodded as he set his heavy backpack on the floor. "I'm afraid she did honey."

Her eyes filled up. "So, she's not comin' to be with us?"

He shook his head.

"Not ever?"

Timothy picked her up and held her tightly. "No, baby, not ever."

"She went to be with daddy, didn't she?"

He slowly nodded his head. "Yes, baby...she did."

Lizbeth laid her head against his chest. "She really missed daddy." Her breath caught, and then she added softly as she cried. "So do I."

"I know sweetheart, I know...The Pinkerton lady told me that she and her friends took care of the bad men that killed your daddy."

Ken Farmer

"She told me they would." She leaned back and asked, "Where are we goin'?"

"We're going to visit your Uncle James at his cabin at Caddo Lake for a while."

"Oh…Haven't seen Unka James in a really long time."

LUCIUS WELLMAN'S CLINIC

Bone and Bodie unloaded Riley and carried him inside.

"In here boys, we'll get him in a bed…I need to clean and stitch that nasty wound on the side of his head…Did a nice job stopping the bleeding."

"Used powdered alum. Marshal Lindsey said he always carried some in his med pouch when he was on the trail…So, we started doing the same," said Loraine. "We get it from the local tonsorial parlor."

"It does a good job," commented Doctor Wellman.

"Is it all right if I stay here with him, Doc?" asked Silke.

"Oh, Miss Justice, I really don't see the point. I don't see any sign that he might wake up anytime soon…which is actually a good thing. The lack of activity will allow a better environment for his brain to heal…I expect Lucy about eleven or so in the morning. Why don't ya'll come back then?"

Silke frowned. "Well, if you think so. I just don't want him wakin' up an' nobody be here."

"I'll be in the next room down the hall…don't worry." He smiled and patted her shoulder.

Silke caressed the side of Riley's face softly. "He looks like he's sleepin'."

"Basically, he is. His body has shut down so the repair can begin."

She nodded and joined Bone, Loraine, and Bodie at the door—Bear Dog at her heels.

They went down the walkway and got back in the carriage.

SKEANS BOARDING HOUSE

Padrino drove the Phaeton the few blocks east to Faye's boarding house and pulled around the back to the carriage house.

"Whoa up there, boys." He eased back on the ribbons.

Silke, Loraine, Bone, Bodie, and Bear Dog all exited.

"I'll help strip the tack from the team, feed an' water 'em, Padrino…Easier two of us doin' it."

"Thanks, Bodie, appreciate it…Hope Faye's got some coffee on," he replied.

"Ever know her not to?" answered Bodie.

"We'll save ya'll some," said Silke as she watched Bear Dog do his business over at the shrubs alongside the yard.

The half-grown, coal-black, wolf-dog scratched the ground with all four feet, and then made a beeline back to Silke.

"Everything come out all right, Bear Dog?" asked Bone.

He spun around twice, woofed at Bone and pranced alongside Silke to the back door of the stately, red brick, Queen Anne style house.

Loraine led the way through the back door into the kitchen where Faye and Annabel were sitting around the table working on their evening coffee.

"You're back," said Faye as she got to her feet, took five cups from the cupboard and set them on the table.

"How did you know, Faye?" asked Loraine.

The attractive, dark blonde-haired widow tilted her head forward and looked at Loraine from under her eyebrows.

"Right," said Loraine.

"Is Ranger Boston goin' to be all right?" asked Annabel.

Silke looked at Bodie's blonde wife for a moment before she replied. "We don't know."

§§§

CHAPTER TWO

GAINESVILLE, TEXAS

"Hey, gotta idea…" said Clay Farmer, City Marshal Ken Farmer's son.

"That's scary," commented Eli Turner, Clay's best friend.

"No, I'm serious," responded Clay.

"That's even scarier," said Daisy Phillips, Clay's girl friend.

Clay looked askance at her. "What say we go on a campin' an' fishin' trip to Lake Caddo over in east Texas to celebrate our graduation?"

The group of high school friends sat around on the big screened-in back porch of Marshal Farmer's house in south Gainesville, two blocks from Skeans Boarding House, drinking lemonade.

They had been close friends since grade school and included Clay, Daisy, Eli, Angel Nelson, her boyfriend, Jed Hackwell, Buck Stienke's daughter, Jen, and Etta Price.

"Farmer, sometimes you actually do come up with a good idea," said the knockout, blonde, Angel.

The others muttered their agreement, except for Eli.

"Taught him everything I know."

"Took you all of two minutes," added Etta, the tall brunette of the bunch.

"Hey, hey, don't pick on the Turner kid." He glanced over at Clay. "Better go ask your dad…He wanted us to paint ya'll's house, you know," said Eli.

"Uh-oh," commented Daisy.

Clay, Eli, and Daisy got up and headed inside the house to Marshal Farmer's study.

"Safety in numbers," mumbled Clay as they walked down the hallway.

Marshal Farmer was sitting in his overstuffed cowhide covered chair, reading his new copy of Sir Arthur Conan Doyle's *The Firm of Girdlestone*.

"Uh...Dad?"

Farmer didn't look up. "What? Can't you see I'm doin' what you should be doin'."

"Huh?"

The intrepid lawman looked up over his wire-rimmed reading glasses. "Readin'...Just because school's out doesn't mean you stop learnin', Boy."

"Oh...yessir."

"Now...what do you want?"

"Well, you see...we...uh...that is, Eli, Daisy, and me...uh, I..."

"Same thing."

"What he's trying to say is, Marshal Farmer...we would like to take the next couple days off and do some campin' an' fishin' down to Lake Caddo...to celebrate the end of school."

"Ya'll really like to push it, don't you?" said the Marshal. "Think the house is goin' to paint itself?"

"We'll get it all painted by the end of next week an' if that ain't a fact...God's a possum," added Eli.

Farmer put his book down in his lap, removed his spectacles, and let his gaze drift over each one of them. "Awright, 'spect Pa'ja-má an' me can do any prep that has to be done...Gonna cost you kids, though."

"What?" asked Clay.

"Let you know when you get back. Have Pa'ja-má make ya'll up some food packs for campin'...Wouldn't trust your ability to catch your dinner."

"Yessir...Thanks, Dad."

"Yeah, right...Ya'll takin' the train, I suppose?"

"Yessir, the Texas an' Pacific goes from Texarkana to Jefferson now...Think it's about fifteen miles from town to the lake."

"Be sure you take a couple of Winchesters with you...an' your Colt...Ya'll know that's the only natural lake in Texas, don't you?"

"Yessir," said Daisy.

"Legend has it it's supposed to be haunted an' have some of those big hairy man-beast creatures the Chickasaw call *Lofa*...I'm told...'Long with the gators."

Clay, Daisy, and Eli exchanged glances.

"Now better get your butts out of here an' get a hurry on if you're goin' to make the east bound."

Daisy pecked the Marshal on the cheek. "Thank you, Papa Ken." She then turned, and the three headed into the kitchen.

"Pa'ja-má, could you make up some food packs?...'Bout seven of us are goin' campin' an' fishin' for the next three days."

The large black woman with a red Aunt Jemima scarf tied around her head, slapped her ample thigh with a dish towel as she turned to face the kids.

"Lawsamercy, chile, it ain't like I gots nothin' else to do, now you want's me to fix up enough foods for seven of you...Want's me to go 'long an' serves you, too?"

Clay wrapped his arms around the woman that virtually raised him since his mother died when he was four. "Pa'ja-ma', you know I love you...You don't want us to go hungry, do you?" He kissed her on the cheek.

She swatted him on the rear with the towel. "Oh, you...Awlays knows how to work pore ol' Pa'ja-má, don'tcha?"

He kissed her on the forehead and smiled.

"There you go, grinnin' like a 'coon eatin' 'simmons...Give me 'bout thirty minutes an' I be bringin' it out to the porch fer ya...Now, scat 'fore I has to go cut me a switch."

He winked at her and said, "Yessum."

SKEANS BOARDING HOUSE

The sun had been up for several hours, warming the spring day.

"I'm goin' on over to Doctor Wellman's. Lucy should be there anytime," said Silke as she got to her feet.

"I'll go with you," commented Bodie as he put his coffee mug on the counter next to the wet sink.

"Us too," added Loraine as she, Bone, and Padrino stood up and also set their cups on the counter.

"Just as well walk, not very far. No need in saddlin' up." Silke pulled her jean jacket from a peg on the wall.

"Oh, Silke, that's a beautiful unique necklace. Get it at the ceremony?" asked Faye, noticing the solid silver crossed tomahawks on the thong around her slim neck.

She nodded. "*Anompoli Lawa* presented me with it after I was inducted into the Hatchet Woman Clan of the Chickasaw."

"Those are the women warriors of the tribe, that go into battle with the men, and sing songs to the enemy, aren't they?"

"Yes...thought that was fascinatin' about them doin' that...an' then takin' their warhawks an' dispatchin' the enemy after they had distracted them," replied Silke.

"That tomahawk they gave her does a job, I'm here to say," said Bone.

Faye looked at the beautiful young woman a long moment.

Silke pursed her lips and nodded as she remembered almost decapitating Duce Walton.

LUCIUS WELLMAN'S CLINIC

Silke, Bone, Loraine, Padrino, and Bodie walked into the front door of the clinic. Nurse Hilda, a heavy set, but pleasant-faced woman of fifty in a white nurse's smock, greeted them.

"Ya'll come in, the doctor is expecting you. He's in the ranger's room with your friend, Lucy and Sheriff Flynn's brother-in-law, Cletus Wilson."

Silke nodded. "We know the way."

She led the group through the door to the hospital area and into Ranger Boston's room.

Lucy, the diminutive pixie-haired, stranded alien masquerading as an Earth child, from the spacecraft crash at Aurora, Texas in 1897, was standing beside Raleigh's bed, she was holding his hand. She looked up as they came in.

"Glad you all are here...Bone, will you assist me?"

"'Course, Lucy, but there's not room on the bed for the both of us."

"That's all right. We can sit in chairs on each side of the bed and hold his hand as I am doing now."

"You're the boss," replied Bone as he carried a slatback chair to the opposite side of Riley's bed.

"You did an excellent job before. Your life energy stopped the bleeding inside his head. I'm not sure how much good we're going to be able to do…I think most of his healing is going to be in the Great Entity's hands, but we'll do what we can," she said.

Silke leaned over to Loraine. "Great Entity?"

"God," she whispered back.

"Ah, of course."

"Lucy's people also believe in a single creator that we call God, Jehovah, Elohim, Yahweh, and so on…To them, the creator is female and is referred to as the Great Entity."

"As you've said before, Loraine, 'a rose by any other name…',￼" responded Silke.

Lucy and Bone had each grasped one of Riley's hands in both of theirs, closed their eyes, and went into the meditative state.

As before, a soft blue glow emanated from the ranger's comatose body and grew stronger over the next several minutes until his body could not be seen.

Loraine turned to Wellman's nurse. "Hilda, would you bring a large pitcher of water and two glasses, please?"

"Of course." She left the room.

Ten minutes later, the glow began to diffuse until it disappeared all together. Both Lucy and Bone's heads dropped to their chests as in deep sleep.

Doctor Wellman took Riley's pulse and looked under each eyelid to check the pupils. "The pupils are better, not quite so dilated."

"But, he's still unconscious," said Silke.

Bone stirred and shook his head, blinked several times and looked around the room. Loraine poured him a full glass of water and handed it to him.

"Thanks, Babe." He took it and drained the glass without taking it from his lips.

Loraine took it from him and filled it again. He nodded and drained it also.

Lucy slowly lifted her head and took a deep cleansing breath. Padrino handed her a full glass, knowing that would be the first thing she required. She drank hers, though not as rapidly as Bone.

Lucy looked over at Riley, released his hand and glanced at Doctor Wellman. "His skull was definitely fractured...but that's healed now. It will take some time for his body to remove the intracranial fluid that had accumulated."

"How long will that be?" asked Silke.

Lucy shook her head. "It's in the hands of the Great Entity now...Bone and I have done all we can...We wait."

§§§

CHAPTER THREE

JEFFERSON, TEXAS
TEXAS & PACIFIC DEPOT

Timothy McPherson stepped down from the passenger car of the Dallas bound train. He held Elizabeth's hand. She carried her small carpet bag and Sally, and he had his backpack slung over his left shoulder.

"How do we get to Unka James's cabin?"

"We'll go down to the livestock car and get my horse, Black Jack. It's about four hours to where he lives."

CADDO LAKE

Elizabeth sat behind her uncle with her arms wrapped around his waist as his black gelding, Black Jack, with one white stocking and a blaze in the middle of his face, trotted along the narrowing trail toward the lake. Sally, her rag doll, was lodged safely between her and the cantle.

Towering cypress trees festooned with long drooping strands of gray Spanish moss became more prevalent the closer they got to the twenty-seven thousand square acre lake. The overall appearance of the area with its still, ominous, black water, interspersed with the huge cypress trees was like something out of primordial history.

Elizabeth looked around as they amble trotted along through the trees with Big Cypress Bayou on their left and the eerie, dark lake on the right.

"Are there ghosts here, Unka Mack?...This really looks spooky."

"Oh, let's hope not, honey...Do you believe in ghosts?"

"Well, mama said that we never really die. That our soul lives forever...an' that not everyone goes to Heaven."

"I suppose that's true...at least for the bad people."

"Like the ones that killed my daddy?"

"I would say...Look! See that log cabin up there through the trees on the other side of that bayou?"

"Uh-huh."

"That's Uncle James's."

They worked their way through the shadowy trees and crossed the narrow bayou where the water came to the horse's belly.

McPherson pulled rein in front of the large cabin, surrounded by cypress trees, located on a spit of land nestled between the bayou and the lake proper.

A log barn was off to the right of the house about ten yards and a boat dock to the left, out into the bayou, with a flat-bottomed pirogue tied to it.

"Hello, the house," yelled Tim as he dismounted and lifted Elizabeth from behind the saddle to the ground.

In a short moment the thick plank door opened and Jim McPherson, his identical twin brother, stepped out onto the wide porch...

SKEANS BOARDING HOUSE

"Suppose I need to get on the trail of McPherson...Can't do much here till Riley wakes up." Silke poured herself a cup of coffee. "No tellin' where he headed since we know he didn't come back to Gainesville..."

"Maybe we do and maybe we don't," commented Bone.

"Oh, what makes you say that?"

"Well, before we loaded up in the carriage, I stepped inside the depot and sent an official sheriff's department telegram back to the KATY depot in Denison inquiring if McPherson booked passage to anywhere...to let me know." He held up a yellow flimsy. "This was waiting when we got back here from the clinic...A little detective work."

"What's it say?" asked Silke.

"Oh, didn't *say* anything," he replied with his enigmatic grin.

"You have my permission to whack him upside the head with your warhawk, Silke...That's just Bone being Bone," commented Loraine.

He giggled. "It *read* that one Timothy McPherson and a girl child booked passage on the Texas and Pacific to Jefferson, Texas."

Silke shook her head and rolled her eyes. Bear Dog looked up at her and cocked his head. "Wonder what's in Jefferson?"

Bone giggled again. "Nothing...But just to the east is an area right out of the Jurassic."

"Excuse me?" Bodie looked at the big man calmly sitting at the table working on a cup of coffee.

"Oh...that's a period in the history of the world about one hundred and fifty million years ago when dinosaurs and the like roamed the planet...It's about 225,000 acres of cypress swamp with a 25 to 30 thousand acre lake in the middle...Swear to God, looks like something from prehistoric times...Caddo Lake."

"Like Jules Verne's, *Journey to the Center of the Earth* he wrote in '64…Read that one too when I was guardin' those gold shipments," said Bodie.

"Oh, yes, heard of that place. People go in there an' don't come out," commented Silke. "Understand it's a haven for outlaws of all stripes."

"It's similar to the Cajun Triangle in Louisiana and the Big Thicket in southeast Texas," said Bone.

"The well known pirate, Jean Lafitte, was said to visit the Caddo Lake area regularly back about eighty or ninety years ago," added Padrino. "Heard it has gators up to almost twenty feet long."

"Plus Bigfoot," said Bone.

"What's a Bigfoot?" Silke questioned.

"The Chickasaw call him *Lofa*…He's a giant man-ape, like we saw up in the Kiamichis with Teddy Roosevelt," said Bodie.

JEFFERSON, TEXAS
TEXAS & PACIFIC DEPOT

The seven friends disembarked from the second southbound train with their camping gear in hand.

Eli carried his guitar, Clay had a SAA Colt .45 strapped around his hips and he, along with Jed, carried Winchester '94s.

"There's the livery stable across the street," said Etta. "Hope they have enough horses."

"Supposed to," replied Clay. "Daddy said he would send a telegram reservin' seven saddle horses plus a pack mule when he went down to the jail."

"If the Marshal said he would, you can carve it in stone," added Angel. "He thinks a liar is no better than a thief."

"Tell me about it," said Clay as he headed across the street. "Worse thrashin' I ever got was when I lied to him about doin' my homework one time."

"Him or Pa'ja-má?" asked Daisy.

"Well, it was Pa'ja-má...Made me go out and cut a peach switch for her...Figured it was better that she administered the punishment 'stead of daddy...Still couldn't sit down for three days."

"Never did it again, didja?" asked Eli.

"Not hardly...Kinda like pickin' up a hot horseshoe."

"Where did she get the name Pa'ja-má?" inquired Jen.

"Yeah, wondered 'bout that my ownself," added Jed.

"Well, her real name is Esmeralda, but she said the other kids never could say it right an' she saw the word *pajama* in the Montgomery Ward catalogue an' thought it was pronounced Pa'ja-má and was real pretty...It stuck." Clay walked through the big double doors of Jason's Livery.

"It is pretty," said Angel as she and the others followed him.

A crusty, skinny older man in worn striped bib overalls over faded red longjohns, wearing a battered brown fedora that had seen better days, stepped out of a stall carrying a four prong pitchfork.

He spat a long stream of amber tobacco juice into the loose hay laying in the aisleway. "You be Marshal Farmer's boy from Gainesville, ain'tcha?"

"Yessir," replied Clay.

"Names' Murphy...Been 'spectin' you...Got yer mounts an' pack mule out in the corral, all tacked out. Jest gotta tighten the cinches up, load the pack mule, an' they be ready to go."

"Thank you, sir," said Daisy. "We appreciate it."

"Now ya'll stay to the trails, don't go wanderin' off, hear?...That lake's tricky, everthin' looks kindly the same...Lots of folks been lost out there an' never heard from agin."

He spat another stream to the side as they started to walk out to the corrals. "Oh, an' a word to the wise...Best picket them animals good at night, er they'll be back here, lickety-split...A bit what I calls *barn sour*...An' you'll be shanks mare."

"Dang sure wouldn't want that," muttered Eli.

"What's that?" asked Murphy as he cupped his hand to his ear.

"Said thought I heard a cat," replied Eli over his shoulder as he followed Clay and the others out to the corral.

Murphy cocked his head, frowned, and glanced around the barn.

Twenty minutes later, the group of intrepid campers had loaded their tents and other camping gear in the panniers on the pack mule, and headed east toward the lake, munching on some sandwiches Pa'ja-má had made for them.

"Need to find a place next to the water to set up camp before sunset," said Clay as he glanced behind him at the sun. "Got about three or so hours before it starts gettin' dark." He pulled out a new pack of Beeman's Black Jack gum, opened a stick and popped it in his mouth.

None of them noticed the blue bank just peeking above the horizon to the northwest or three rough-looking men watching them leave...

CADDO LAKE

"Hello, brother, didn't expect to see you until next week," said Jim as he hugged his twin.

"Had a little change in plans...You remember Elizabeth? Sarah's daughter?"

"My, but you've grown, dear," he said as he knelt down and hugged her too. "How's your mama an' them?"

She looked up at her Uncle Mack and then looked down at the ground.

"They're both gone, Jim," replied Timothy.

Jim pursed his lips and looked off to the west. "We best put your horse up in the barn and get inside...Looks like there's a storm brewing."

§§§

CHAPTER FOUR

SKEANS BOARDING HOUSE
GAINESVILLE, TEXAS

"Well, guess we ought to head over to Jefferson tomorrow," said Bone.

"What's wrong with today?" asked Silke.

"One, there's no trains running east this late and two, my knee's barking at me...Storm coming."

"You sure?" Silke asked.

"Go look out the front window to the west."

Silke got up from the dark green settee in the parlor, walked over to one of the front windows and pulled the curtain back. "Oh, my." She looked at the dark blue line off to the northwest.

"Think we have time to go down to the Painted Lady for a beer before it hits?...Like to nose around, see if anyone has heard from McPherson."

"Good idea, Bone," commented Loraine.

"You stay put, mister," Annabel said to her husband, Bodie, as he started to get up.

"What?" He looked at her.

"We have somethin' to talk about."

Bodie glanced at the others. "Uh-oh."

Bone grinned. "Believe I'd do what she said, Bodie."

PAINTED LADY SALOON

Twenty minutes later Silke, Bone, Loraine, and Padrino walked into the Painted Lady, found a table and took seats.

The late afternoon crowd was growing. A haze of cigarette and cigar smoke was already building just below the fourteen foot ceiling.

Their favorite bar girl, Brandi, approached their table. She was wearing the required costume for waitstaff in the saloon, a typical low-cut saloon girl outfit—even though none of the girls worked upstairs in the Chickasaw Bordello. The costumes were just for atmosphere.

The Painted Lady was an upscale saloon and restaurant patterned after Wyatt Earp's Oriental Saloon in Tombstone in 1880, including a stage for performers.

It did, however, have its share of local cowboys from the numerous surrounding cattle and horse ranches plus the passing through drifters—a number of which were lined up at the thirty-five foot long San Francisco style bar.

The tall brunette looked over the four regular customers. "What are we havin'?…As if I have to ask."

"Yes," replied Loraine, smiling.

"What I thought." Brandi returned the smile as she turned on her heel and headed back to the bar.

One of the cowboys at the bar grabbed her as she walked up and started to place the order with Rube Jolley, the heavyset forty something bartender.

"Hey, pretty, how's 'bout a kiss?" He leaned forward and tried to kiss Brandi on the lips.

"Let me go." She tried to push the big man away.

"Aw, come on, baby, just one."

"I said let me go."

"Here we go." Bone started to get to his feet.

"Oh, I hate this." Silke interrupted him before he could rise with her hand on his shoulder. "Got it."

She made her way to the bar and grabbed the cowboy's hand that was wrapped around Brandi's arm. "That's not very polite."

The rough-looking cowboy with a week's growth of beard, turned to Silke. "Well, well, sweet thing, you want some of Big Dick Barton?...An' I'm called that for more than one reason." He winked at her.

"Not in this lifetime...Your breath smells like something crawled in your mouth an' died...Plus, I dont' like rude...I detest rude."

Silke kneed him sharply in the crotch causing the big man to wheeze his fetid breath out, grab his bruised privates and bend over. She quickly pinched his lower lip between her thumb and forefinger of her left hand and pulled his face back up level with hers. Silke already had her Chickasaw warhawk in her right.

Barton's eyes got big as saucers and crossed as she brought the razor-sharp blade close to his nose.

"Now, buttercup, I'm goin' to teach you some manners…an' make you more presentable at the same time…No charge. 'Course won't help your odor much."

Silke turned his face to the side, placed the edge of the tomahawk against his scruffy cheek just in front of his ear and started to pull down. The nasty, curly brown stubble piled up in front of the blade on the first audible pass.

"Ah…ah…ah," he managed to squeak out as she made another pass, and then moved over under his nose and scraped the mustache away to fall to the sawdust covered floor.

It only took four more passes with the deadly weapon to finish his face before she lifted up on his lip to lean his head back to shave his neck.

His eyes got even bigger as she scraped the hair away from his throat. He swallowed once, causing his Adams apple to bob—her tomahawk took a small chunk of flesh from the top.

"Wouldn't do that again, were I you."

The blood trickled down onto his red bandanna.

Silke turned his face from side to side and inspected her work. She looked over at Loraine.

"What do you think, Deputy?"

"Missed some under his lower lip, I think," Loraine said.

"Oh, yeah." She released his lip and grabbed the end of his nose, tweaked it, and cleaned up the area below his lower lip and his chin. "How's that?"

"Looks good...What about a haircut?" asked Bone.

Barton shook his head. "No, please...I'll be good, honest Injun, I will."

Silke turned his nose loose. "Now apologize to the lady." She indicated Brandi.

Barton jerked his Montana pinch creased hat from his head and held it in front of him, crushing it to his chest.

"Ma'am, I'm powerful sorry. Won't happen again."

"You'll leave a nice tip, won't you?" said Silke. "And be a good boy?"

"Oh, yes, ma'am…count on that."

"I'll be watchin'." Silke twirled the warhawk through her fingers, and then slipped it back into her belt. She turned and sashayed back to their table.

Rube put ol' Betsy, his well-worn baseball bat, back under the bar. He had pulled it out just before Silke took care of the situation.

"Dang, girl, you're 'bout half-dangerous aren't you?" said Bone as Silke sat back down.

"Learned a lot from Loraine."

"You were nicer than I would have been." Lorained grinned. "But, I think you made your point."

They looked up as Brandi approached the table with a small round tray with four long necks on it—two Lone Star and two Pearl. She set the Lone Stars in front of Bone and Padrino and the Pearls with Loraine and Silke.

"On the house." She looked at Silke. "And thank you…That was about the neatest thing I've seen since you and Loraine worked over that group of toughs the last time ya'll were in."

"Say, Brandi, where's Mister McPherson?" asked Silke as she turned her bottle up and took a sip.

"Went huntin', he said."

"Heard from him?" inquired Bone.

She paused and cocked her head. "Now that you mention it...no, don't think so. I'll ask Rube...Mister McPherson always puts him in charge when he's gone...Be back in a shake."

Brandi turned and meandered her way through the tables back to the bar.

"Mind if I join you?" Marshal Farmer limped up to their table.

"'Course not, have a chair," said Bone.

Farmer pulled out one of the bow chairs, leaned his bull penis cane against the side of the table and sat down as Brandi brought a Budweiser and set it in front of him.

"Saw you come in, Marshal." Brandi glanced over at Silke and grinned. "You missed the show."

He looked at Silke, and then over at the bar at the big cowboy with the bright red, freshly scraped face with little spots of blood showing and his bandanna wrapped a little higher on his neck.

47

"Darn, hate that." He grinned at Silke, and lifted his Bud up for a long swallow, then turned to her. "Rude, huh?…Probably owe you some thanks, Detective."

Silke grinned and nodded. "All in a day's work." She took another sip of her beer.

"I would have been here in time to see it, but got a late start. Had to make arrangements for my son and his friends to go on a campin' an' fishin' trip."

"How many went?" inquired Loraine.

"Seven, all together."

"Where'd they go?" asked Padrino.

"Caddo Lake."

Bone and the others exchanged glances.

"You don't say?" said Silke.

Farmer nodded. "Took the afternoon train…I arranged for horses and a pack mule in Jefferson for 'em."

"Know where they're goin' to be?" asked Loraine.

"Nope…Big place, I hear…Just gonna be next to the water, though."

"Ever been there?" Padrino looked over at the lawman.

"Nope, never have."

"It's like something out of time's abyss," said Bone.

"Really?"

"Kid you not." Bone turned his Lone Star up and drained it in one fell swoop as the distant peal of thunder sounded.

"Expect we best drink up, folks, and head back to the house since we're walking," said Padrino.

Thunder rolled again as the outside got darker as the clouds covered the late afternoon sun.

The fresh smell of the coming rain wafted into the saloon from the big open clerestory windows across the front of the building just under the fourteen foot high tin ceiling.

"Think it's goin' to be a dandy." Silke finished her Pearl.

"Dang, hope the kids get their camp an' tents set up 'fore the storm gets there." Farmer listened to the thunder rumble overhead like God was moving furniture around.

Fifteen minutes later, Silke, Bone, Loraine, and Padrino ran up the flagstone walkway to the wide wraparound porch of the boarding house just as dime-sized drops of rain began to splatter down with audible impact sounds.

CADDO LAKE

"Wind's pickin' up, better hurry." Clay drove the last tent peg into the ground with a rock.

"Yeah, that line of storms is definitely gettin' closer," agreed Eli as he dumped a load of firewood under another tent to keep it dry.

They had crossed Big Cypress Bayou, made camp on some high ground known as Horse Island and pitched their three tents.

Clay and Daisy were in one, Angel and Jed in another with Eli, Etta, and Jen in the third. The horses and mule were staked out on some spring grass and clover back toward the bayou just this side of the narrow strip of land they used to get to the island.

Lightening flashed nearby accompanied by a loud clap of thunder.

"Let's all get in our tent till after the storm, it's big enough," said Clay. "Put the supplies in the others along with the firewood."

"Good idea, O' great leader." Eli bowed.

The three rough-looking, butt-ugly men, dressed like woodsmen, watched the group from some bushes near the bayou.

"Let's git to our cabin till the storm passes...They ain't goin' nowheres," said the leader, Cobb.

"You see them gals? They's four of 'em...I git the blonde," commented Polk.

"You git who I say," snapped Cobb. "Might even give you one of them boys."

"Hey, I'll take the chunky one...he's purty." Marvin grinned, showing three of his front teeth missing.

He spat a stream of watery snuff juice to the side, and then wiped the dribble from his chin with the sleeve of his tattered shirt.

Marvin, soon's they git inside that tent, you slip over to their animals an' cut them picket lines."

Cobb chuckled. "Dollar to a bear sign they'll haul-ass back to the livery when the storm hits."

§§§

CHAPTER FIVE

SKEANS BOARDING HOUSE

The lightning flashed and the thunder roared with a staccato regularity almost nonstop like an artillery exchange bombardment.

The double-hung float glass windows of the stately three story Queen Anne style house rattled like tambourines with each clap of thunder.

Bear Dog crawled under the coffee table in the parlor and crossed his paws over his nose each time the thunder rolled.

"Don't think he likes the thunder much," said Bone as he and the others hung their jackets on the hall tree in the foyer.

"I think it hurts his ears…Much more sensitive than ours," replied Silke as she got down on her knees, reached under the table and caressed the top of his coal-black head. "It's all right, boy."

Annabel was also in the floor playing with her and Bodie's twins, Bass and Cassie Ann, while he sat on the settee drinking a cup of coffee. He was grinning like a Cheshire cat.

Loraine looked over at Bodie. "Well, you look like you had a big slice of buttermilk pie."

He nodded and grinned even bigger.

"Are you going to tell us or do I have to get my sweet Loraine to beat the stuffin' out of you?" said Bone.

Bodie glanced down at Annabel and the twins. "Bass an' Cassie Ann are goin' to have a little brother or sister."

"A new baby?…That's wonderful," commented Silke as she rushed over and hugged his neck.

"Ya'll figure out what caused it, yet?" asked Padrino as he came back from the kitchen with a cup of coffee.

"No, but we got some ideas," Bodie responded.

"Mister…" Annabel warned. "Don't overload your wagon…act like you got some sense. Hate to peel your head like a onion."

"Yessum." He ducked his head and grinned again as an extra loud clap of thunder followed right on the heels of a tremendous flash of lightning.

Everyone in the room jumped while Bear Dog whined.

"Dang, I hate lightnin'," exclaimed Bodie. "Annabel wants me to take her an' the kids to Alabama to see the grandparents 'fore she gets too big to travel…We can take the train all the way to Mobile."

"Sounds like ya'll'll be gone 'bout three weeks or so," commented Silke from her spot on the floor next to the coffee table.

"Ever bit of it…Sorry I won't be able to go after McPherson an' that little girl with ya'll." He looked over at his wife and smiled. "I got my marchin' orders whilst ya'll were at the Painted Lady."

Another lightning flash and tremendous clap of thunder shook the house.

Bear Dog crawled out from under the table, pointed his black nose in the air and let loose a long howl. He turned his blue eyes to Silke's, that were almost the same shade of blue as his, but were surrounded with dark, long lashes, seeking comfort.

The four year old twins both giggled at Bear Dog, and then they grabbed him around the neck for a group hug. He responded to the babies with multiple kisses to their cherubic faces.

"Ya'll have a good time…Think we've got it covered anyway…Have to go up tomorrow for Red Wolf's funeral before we go after McPherson," she responded to Bodie. "When ya'll leavin'?"

"In the mornin'…East bound leaves at nine."

Silke looked at Bone. "You know when the train to Ardmore leaves?"

"Ten, last time I checked."

She nodded. "Have time to go check on Riley."

Thunder rolled again.

SILKE'S QUEST

CADDO LAKE

The wall of rain hit Clay's tent like a freight train. The girls hugged each other while the boys tried to keep the bottom down on the windward side.

Eli peeked through the narrow slit in the front flap that he was trying to hold together.

"Jumpin' JimBobs, it's rainin' sideways. Can't see two feet."

The sound of the storm changed as hail began to pepper the canvas.

They looked up at the angled top of the military tent, and then at each other as the hail sounded like multiple Gatlin Guns firing at the same time—the roar was deafening, making communication almost impossible.

Lightning flashes and claps of thunder were nonstop.

Everyone put their hands over their ears.

Clay yelled at the top of his lungs, "Who's bright idea was this, anyway?"

The others just pointed their fingers at him.

"Fear not, my son, this too shall pass," Eli screamed back.

"Hell you say," hollered Daisy as she pulled a blanket over her head.

Then, just as quickly as the storm had begun, it stopped, except for the water dripping from the roof of the tent, the trees, and Spanish moss nearby.

Eli stuck his head through the flap at the front. "Holy crap," he exclaimed.

"What is it? asked Angel.

"We're surrounded."

"Do what?" inquired Jed.

Eli looked back at the others. "We're on a real island. That trail we came across, is now under water…We're surrounded by water…Oh, an' the horses an' mule are gone."

"What do you mean, 'gone'?" asked Clay.

"G-O-N-E…Gone. Not there anymore, vanished, disappeared, vamoosed…What part of that don't you understand?"

"They can't be," said Etta. "We picketed them good."

"Tell them that," replied Eli as he untied the strings that held the flaps together. "Gotta pee like a pet coon."

He stepped outside followed by the others.

"Go ahead, we won't watch," commented Daisy.

"I will," replied Jen.

"Bite me," he said back to her as he walked toward a big cottonwood, stepping over the plethora of limbs scattered about the ground.

They surveyed the area around the camp. One of the tents had collapsed on top of the supplies and there were branches, limbs and marble-sized hail stones piled everywhere.

"Yep, the animals are gone...I'll be damned," said Clay.

"What did I say?" replied Eli as he shook the last drops off, put his equipment away, and was buttoning his trousers up while he turned back around from the tree. "Thought I was jerkin' your rope, didn'tcha?"

"Sorry," replied Clay. "Just didn't think they could break loose."

He walked over to where they had picketed them and picked up one of the ropes still tied to the stake in the ground.

"By the Lord Jim..."

"What is it?" asked Jed as he walked over also.

Clay looked at him, and then the others as he held up the end of the rope. "This was cut...it didn't break."

"So is this one," added Jed as he picked another one up. "They all are."

"Somebody wants us stranded out here," said Daisy.

They looked around at the deepening shadows of the surrounding Spanish moss draped woods and the black water of the lake, and then exchanged glances...

"Best we get a fire goin', not gonna be a moon till after midnight," said Clay.

"Yeah, gonna be black as three feet up a bull's butt till then."

"How do you know how dark it is up in there, Eli?" asked Angel.

"Jen told me," he replied, and then forgot to duck as she bounced a downed branch off his head.

"Ow, you coulda hurt me, Jen." He rubbed the back of his head.

"Not likely...Hit you in the head."

"Ha-ha."

They were unaware of the dark brown eyes watching them from the brush in the gloaming...

Clay turned around to look over the rest of camp and noticed the collapsed tent was moving.

"What the..." He drew his Colt.

The others also turned. They saw a white hand sneak out from between the slit at what was apparently the front of the tent. Then the arm showed followed by a red plaid shirt clad shoulder.

They exchanged looks and moved closer to the downed tent.

A girl's head, festooned with flaming red hair, with a long single loose braid tied at the bottom with a leather thong was looped over her left shoulder. Her hair was frizzy from the heavy humidity following the rain.

The attractive sixteen year old turned, and they could see her striking green-eyes surrounded by alabaster skin, and a pert nose sprinkled with a blanket of freckles.

The girl worked her upper body out, stood to her feet and pushed the rest of the tent down her fitted bib overalls with the legs tucked into tall lace-up boots like she was stepping out of a couture dress.

There was a leather belt around her hips, just below her wasp waist, with a ten inch bone-handled Bowie and a tomahawk stuck in it.

"Wow, first time I ever saw a tent give birth," said Jed.

She smiled, showing a row of even white teeth, first at Eli, and then at the others. "Hi."

"Who are you?" asked Eli.

"Maggie...my daddy calls me the Cat...Who are ya'll?"

Clay handled the introductions for everybody.

"Thanks for the loan of your tent. I smelled the hail comin' an' just made it 'fore it hit."

"You can smell hail?" asked Daisy.

"Sure, just like you can smell rain comin'...I can smell hail, too...Say, think we can start a fire with the dry wood under this tent...'fore it gets completely dark? I got a little rained on."

"Sure...Let me stand that thing back up an' we can do just that," said Clay as he holstered his Colt.

"What are you doin' out here?" asked Angel.

"Could ask ya'll the same..." She held up a sack, made out of burlap, that was looped across her chest from her left shoulder. "Out huntin' alligator an' snappin' turtle eggs."

"Really?" inquired Etta.

"Uh-huh…Good eatin'. Only take a couple from each nest…Mama gators will follow me if I take more…Kinda testy 'bout their babies."

"You're kiddin'," said Eli.

"Nope…"

"You don't carry a gun?" asked Jen.

"Don't need one…This is my swamp…know it like the back of my hand…Say, ya'll know the shiners 'er watchin' ya'll…don'tcha?"

They looked at each other. "Shiners?" most of them said simultaneously…

§§§

CHAPTER SIX

CADDO LAKE

Elizabeth held tightly to her uncle Timothy as they sat on the brown leather couch inside his brother, James's, spacious log cabin. She flinched at each clap of thunder and held tighter to her uncle.

"It's going to be all right, honey," he said as he comforted her.

The storm raged outside while the hail drummed down on the standing seam metal roof like a hundred locomotives charging along the tracks.

James, Timothy, and Elizabeth looked up at the ceiling as the storm moved on to the southeast and the roar subsided to an eerie quiet.

Elizabeth looked at Timothy. "Is it over, Unka Mack?"

"I think so, honey."

"Wish Margaret was here." She nestled her head against his shoulder.

James and Timothy exchanged quick glances.

"So do I, Elizabeth," he replied.

She glanced out the window at the rain drops still on the panes of glass, and the darkness beyond.

Elizabeth's face opened into a big yawn as she laid her head back over on McPherson's shoulder.

"I think I know somebody that's ready for bed," said James. "Come on in here, she can sleep in Margaret's room."

He got to his feet, picked up one of the burning coal-oil lamps in the room, and led the way to a doorway on the south side of the big main room.

Timothy tucked her into bed and kissed her forehead. The two men exited the room and closed the door behind them.

"Now, want to fill me in, brother?" said James.

Thirty minutes later over glasses of Kentucky Bourbon, Timothy brought his twin up to speed on the situation.

James, downed the rest of his drink and shook his head. "Told you not to hire that Walton fellow…A known killer. Too easy for 'em to do what they've done before."

SKEANS BOARDING HOUSE

Silke pulled the curtains aside from one of the windows at the front of the parlor. "Rain's stopped, but it's black as a banker's heart out there."

"Will be till after midnight," replied Bone.

"I really wanted to walk over to Doctor Wellman's to see Riley…"

"He would have already closed down, Silke. I know, I spent over a month in there when I got shot a while back," offered Bodie. "He's well taken care of...believe me."

"I know, but still the same..."

"We'll go first thing in the morning before we have to catch the train to Ardmore," said Loraine.

"I suppose." Silke frowned and looked outside again.

CADDO LAKE

The fire gave out warming heat and enough light to reach almost to the edge of the clearing. Everyone sat around the blaze with cups of after dinner coffee.

"Now, what are those shiners, you mentioned, Maggie?" asked Clay.

She kept her voice low, causing the others to scoot a little closer to the willowy teen. "Who...It's a clan of moonshiners...'bout fifteen or so all together. Got four stills scattered about the swamp...Me and daddy think they're mostly inbreds..."

"Inbreds?" asked Eli. "Like hillbillies?"

"Pretty much, I'd say…Ugly as burnt boots, the most of 'em…an' dumb as a barrel of hair."

"Hey, you'd fit right in, Eli," said Jen.

"Least I know a widget from a whangdoodle, Stienke," he quipped back.

"What's a whangdoodle?" she asked.

"Haw…See?"

Maggie leaned forward, grabbed the coffee pot handle with her folded over bandanna and refilled her cup. "But, they are dangerous, make no mistake about it…Right an' wrong don't mean much to 'em." She licked the edge of her cup to cool it and took a sip. "Been lots a folks come in these swamps…an' just plain ol' disappear."

"What do you mean, 'disappear'?" asked Daisy.

"Well, word has it that the shiners catch 'em, use the women for a while…an' then feed them an' the men to their hogs…Nobody's ever found any trace of them's that's missin'."

"Ooooh…ugh," said Etta.

"Eli, you an' Jed keep one of the Winchesters with you at all times…I got my Colt," commented Clay.

"Maybe it's the gators," suggested Angel.

Maggie shook her head. "Uh-uh...Gators will always leave somethin'...like the head or a foot which will eventually float...Bear an' panther will leave most of the bones."

"But, how long have you lived in the swamp?" asked Etta.

"Most all my life...so far. I can smell 'em...Gotta real funny scent...How I knew they were watchin' ya'll."

The group looked out into the blackness, and then back at Maggie.

"Uh...What about the *Lofa*?" asked Clay.

"Excuse me?" Maggie asked as she looked over at him.

"The hairy man-beast things that are supposed to be here," said Daisy. "The Chickasaw call them *Lofa*."

"Oh, the creatures with big feet," Maggie responded. "Never seen one, but I have seen their tracks." She held up her hands about twenty inches apart. "They're about this long and yea wide." She indicated about seven inches. "Way too long to be a bear...Plus, don't show claws like bear track."

"Really?" asked Angel.

"Saw a bunch of the prints one time over on the east side of the lake. It was a family of 'em…They were apparently diggin' mussels out of the shallow water, bustin' 'em open with rocks, an' eatin' the meat."

She reached into her possibles pouch, took a handful of blue and wine pearls out and held out her palm.

"They threw these away along with the shells on the bank."

"Golly, those are fresh water pearls," exclaimed Eli.

"Found a bunch of 'em…Here…one for each of you…blue for the boys." Maggie giggled. "An'…wine for the girls." She handed them out.

"Wow, thanks, Maggie, that's very nice," said Daisy as she looked at the pearl in her hand, and then put it in her pocket.

The black, still, night air was abruptly pierced by a high-pitched, bloodcurdling, woman-like scream.

Every cup of coffee in camp, save Maggie's, was sloshed and spilled.

Jen jumped to her feet with a scream of her own.

"Just a panther," Maggie said calmly.

"*Just* a panther?" questioned Etta. She looked to her right. "If we all get killed out here, Clay Farmer...I'm never speakin' to you again."

"I'll make a note of that," he replied. "Let's take turns at night guard...Jed, you take first shift, Eli relieves you at midnight...I'll relieve Eli at three...Stay alert an' keep the fire an' the coffee pot goin'."

"Say, that's a pretty good idea there, great leader," commented Eli.

"Better than you know," added Maggie.

"You can share a tent with me an' Clay, Maggie, it's the biggest. Don't have any blankets, do you?" asked Daisy.

She grinned. "Not hardly...Didn't anticipate the storm comin' up so quick."

"We've got extras," said Clay. "Where's ya'll's cabin?"

"'Bout two an' a half miles to the east. It's out on a narrow spit of land into the middle of the lake on the other side of Big Cypress Bayou."

"How do you get to it? Is there a bridge?" asked Angel.

Maggie laughed. "No bridge...We wade across...Only 'bout four feet deep."

"What about the gators?" asked Eli.

She grinned at him. "You hurry."

"Joy."

"Say, Maggie, how do those shiners make a livin'?... Just sellin' white lightnin'?" asked Eli.

"Uh-uh...They also sell side meat, hams an' sausage in town at the farmer's market," said Maggie.

"From the pigs it's believed they feed people to?" asked Daisy.

Maggie looked at Daisy, and then the others, cocked her right eyebrow and shrugged. "What do you think?"

A three-quarter gibbous moon had risen just above the tree line casting long eerie shadows through the Spanish moss. It was enough light for Marvin, Polk, and Cobb to rig their snares for any wayward passerbys on the narrow game trail.

Cobb spread the hemp loop on the trail and covered it up with dead leaves.

Marvin pulled the black gum sapling down and tied the end of the rope to near the top, while Polk rigged a thin trip wire across the trail.

Any person passing along the trail that hit the trip wire would release the tie-down hold for the sapling. They would be instantly snatched up into the air upside down by the ground loop around their foot.

"Well, that be three of 'em we gots set...Oughta fetch somethin', ye figger?" questioned Polk.

"Got that swamp gal with 'em now...Been wantin' to git me some of that...Ain't seen her in a spell," said Cobb.

"Not much meat on 'er," commented Marvin.

"You know what daddy used to say...Nearer the bone, the sweeter the meat." Cobb chuckled.

"I'll go turn them cottonmouths we catched aloose in they camp...Oughta git 'em a runnin', I mind," added Marvin.

"Ain't no flies on you, brother," said Cobb. "You be makin a hornet look cuddly."

Marvin spat a long stream of viscous tobacco juice to the side and chuckled. "Am smart, ain't I?"

"As a hooty owl," said Polk. "An' you usually ain't worth spit."

"Don't need none of yer mouth, neither, Polk. Knock you plumb into next week."

"You an' who else?" Polk squared away in front of Marvin and brought both fists up like the picture of John L. Sullivan.

"Awright, that's enough. You two ijits make enough noise to wake up everbody in three counties…We needs fresh meat…Now keep it down," said Cobb with a sneer.

§§§

CHAPTER SEVEN

LUCIUS WELLMAN'S CLINIC

Silke sat down beside Riley's bed. She reached over and took his hand in both of hers for a moment, and then released her left and placed it on the side of his face. Silke softly caressed his still face, feeling the four days of stubble that had grown since he had last shaved.

"Shave you when I get back. You rest now an' I'll see you soon," she whispered in his ear and gently kissed his cheek.

Bone, Loraine, and Padrino stood respectfully at the door for Silke's time with the comatose Texas Ranger.

She stood up from the chair she was sitting in, wiped a tear from her eye with the tips of her fingers, looked at him a moment longer, and then turned to join Bone and Loraine.

"Guess we better go," she said softly.

Loraine put her arms around Silke and gave her a good hug. "He's going to be all right, honey, just have faith."

"I know how you feel, Silke. Felt the same way when my sweet Loraine was shot…There's something about that other level of emotion that comes when it's someone you love."

Silke looked up at the big man. "But, I…"

"Hey, you're not kidding anyone but yourself, young lady, if you're saying you're not in love with Riley Boston. You might as well try to hide under a basket…Everybody else already knows," said Loraine smiling.

Silke smiled and kissed her on the cheek. "Thank you." She glanced over at Bone. "The both of you."

Bone shook his head. "Been there…Done that."

He turned and led the way out the door to the carriage.

Padrino picked up the ribbons after the others had gotten in. "Come up there, boys." He flicked the reins over their rumps.

The matched set of standardbreds moved off at a high-stepping single-foot in the direction of the Santa Fe Depot.

Padrino pulled rein in front of the two story wooden shiplap building. "Whoa up there, boys," he said as he eased back on the reins.

Silke, Bone, and Loraine stepped down to the curb.

"We'll try to make the late afternoon train back…If we're lucky," said Bone.

"Should…The service is at eleven," commented Silke.

"See you then," replied Padrino as he flicked the reins over the rumps of the sorrels and cherked at them. "Come up, boys."

Silke, Bone, and Loraine boarded the train after they had purchased their tickets and took seats in the second passenger car.

The engineer released the tall Johnson bar, putting the big 4x4x2 coal-fired locomotive in gear. She chugged, the wheels lost purchase on the steel rails for a short moment, but caught on the second revolution.

The eight car train slowly gained speed, belching a voluminous column of black smoke from her stack as she overcame the inertia of the thousands of pounds of steel and headed north.

Seven miles north of Gainesville, the train sped over the iron bridge that spanned the sluggish Red River that separated Texas from the Indian Nations.

Silke, Bone, and Loraine were seated at the end of the car. Silke was facing forward while Bone and Loraine were in the rear facing seats directly across from her.

The train climbed the shallow grade from the Red River valley into the Chickasaw Nation, the cars rocking from side to side over the uneven rails.

A man in a rumpled three piece dark suit seated in the forward most rear facing seat rose with his Colt in his hand. He discharged a round through the ceiling of the rail car to get everyone's attention.

"Awright folks, this is a holdup…Now, don't nobody do anything stupid an' nobody'll get hurt. I'm gonna pass a flour sack down the aisle, just put your valuables an' guns in it."

He pointed his pistol at a woman on the opposite side of the aisle. "Hate to have to shoot this woman just because of some wannabe hero."

The woman screamed and fell to her right in a swoon.

"What the…" the robber exclaimed as he glanced down at the unconscious woman slumped against the man seated next to her.

His gun, in his right hand across his body, was still pointed down at her.

Suddenly he screamed in pain as the spike end of a Chickasaw warhawk embedded itself in the back of his wrist right in the center of the eight carpal bones. The spike severed the carpal nerve causing the man to loose his grip and drop the Colt.

He fell to his knees, holding his wrist, moaning in pain. Silke, followed by Bone moved quickly down the aisleway. She retrieved his gun as Bone pulled him to his feet and jerked Silke's tomahawk from his wrist, eliciting another wail of pain from the would-be tobyman.

"Nice throw, Silke," Bone said as he wiped the blood from the spike on the man's coat and handed the weapon back to her.

She grinned as she stuck it back into her beaded leather belt. "Figured it was safer for everyone else in the car than blowin' his hand off with my .50 cal you gave me."

"Point there," he replied as the blue clad conductor burst through the rear door of the car and rapidly strode forward.

"What's all this?" he asked.

"This nabob decided he would relieve everyone in the car of any excess valuables and Miss Justice of the Pinkerton National Detective agency took umbrage…and planted a tomahawk in his arm from back down the way," commented Bone.

The conductor turned toward the rear of the car and saw Loraine, who waved at him. "From all the way down there?" he asked with a great deal of incredulity.

Bone nodded.

"Unbelievable," he said softly.

Silke unloaded the man's .45, dropped the remaining four rounds in the floor and handed the weapon to the conductor who stuck it in his waistband.

"Come on, you." He grabbed the whining robber's collar and pushed him down the aisleway toward the rear of the car. "Lock you up in the caboose till we stop at Ardmore...Sure Marshal Lindsey will be glad to take you over."

"Ain't nobody gonna do nothin' 'bout my arm 'fore I bleed to death?"

"Probably not...Shouldn't have tried to rob these folks," said the conductor as they disappeared through the door.

"You're pretty handy with that hatchet, girl," said Bone as they made their way back to their seats.

"Red Wolf, bless his soul, taught me," she replied.

CADDO LAKE

The kids were stirring about the camp, having finished their breakfast and were on their second cup of coffee.

"Is one of us gonna walk back toward town an' see if the horses stopped or anything?" asked Etta.

"Not likely…Those horses an' your mule probably didn't stop till they got back to their barn durin' the storm," said Maggie.

"Figure somebody will come lookin' for us," commented Clay. "I say we start doin' what we came for."

Eli frowned. "An' that was?"

"Catch some fish, numbnuts."

"Oh, that too," he replied.

From their hiding place behind a copse of cedar trees across the narrow causeway that now separated Horse Island from the mainland, Marvin, Polk, and Cobb watched the kids sitting by the fire drinking their coffee.

Marvin held a tow sack by the neck—it contained eight, full grown, deadly cottonmouth moccasins. He shook the bag up and down for a couple of minutes.

"Heh, heh, heh." He spat a stream of brown tobacco juice to the side. "That oughta piss 'em off some," he said. "They're agonna chase anythin' they see movin'."

He moved out from behind the grove of trees, swung the bag around his head several times and slung it toward the middle of the camp.

The sack sailed through the air and landed with a thump on the ground. The eight very angry, aggressive, venomous, pit vipers poured out of the open end of the sack.

Angel was the first to see the dark reptiles wriggling in their direction and screamed.

Every one, but Clay, took off running in different directions. Jed and Etta sloshed across the causeway and headed into the cypress trees on the mainland.

Clay drew his Colt, blew one in half, then shot the head off another as it reared up to strike at him. The bullet entered the center of the trademark white inside of its mouth, exploding its head.

Eli grabbed up one of the Winchesters and shot another that was headed for Daisy.

Angel jumped up on top of a cypress stump that wasn't nearly high enough.

Clay drilled the snake that was raising up to strike at her ankle, blowing the viper in two pieces.

Maggie grabbed one deftly by the tail, snapped it like a bull whip, popping its head from the body.

Jen had picked up a long limb and beat another to a pulp.

"Think you can stop now, Jen," said Eli as the deadly reptile looked like it had been trampled by a horse.

"Hate snakes…Hate 'em," she said as she whacked it one more time.

The other two remaining snakes made their way to the water, slithered in and disappeared in its blackness.

"Everybody all right?" asked Clay.

"Where's Jed an' Etta?" asked Angel looking around.

Her question was answered by a piercing scream from woods across the causeway…

ARDMORE TRAIN DEPOT

Silke, Loraine, and Bone disembarked and were met by Doctor Winchester Ashalatubbi, also known by his Chickasaw tribal name of *Anompoli Lawa* - He Who Talks to Many.

He was a licensed medical doctor, a doctor of divinity, as well as being the Shaman of the Chickasaw Nation.

The white-haired spiritual leader led them to his carriage. "The services are being held at my home before we take Red Wolf out to our sacred burial mound site. No white person may enter or even know its location."

"We understand, Doctor Ashalatubbi,' said Bone.

Anompoli Lawa pulled rein outside a large white clapboard house with a wide front porch. There were many wagons, buggies, and horses tied around the home.

From a group of women on the porch came the mournful Chickasaw death chant.

Red Wolf's body lay in a very ornate beaded white doeskin burial pouch made for him by the women of the tribe, on top of a large table underneath a red oak tree.

The Shaman had sanctified the remains and painted his face ocher, according to Chickasaw custom, before he went to the station to pick up Silke, Bone, and Loraine.

Anompoli Lawa, now also in ceremonial white doeskin with three eagle tail feathers stuck vertically in his bun at the back of his head, pulled out a small beaded pouch from his medicine bag, opened it, took a pinch of sacred dogwood pollen, and scattered it to the four directions. He took another pinch and sprinkled it over the burial pouch and yet another straight up into the air to sanctify the journey to the happy hunting grounds.

He then took his personal totem, carved from a piece of lightning-riven oak, from his medicine bag. *Anompoli Lawa* waved it above the remains, raised his other hand and chanted in the Chickasaw tongue, *"Ababinili-hoyo-aboha-ona Nashoba Hommá. Chihóa-bia-chee*…May the Great Spirit guide you, Red Wolf, that you may achieve your rest…Go with God."

The other tribal members repeated, *"Chihóa-bia-chee, Nashoba Hommá."*

The women of the tribe began to sing softly, a hymn—in the Chickasaw tongue.

Loraine nudged Bone. "That's *Amazing Grace*, I recognize the melody...but it's in the Chickasaw tongue...It's unbelievably beautiful."

Anompoli Lawa overheard her comment and leaned closer. "We have sung that song for strength and at all burial ceremonies since our people were marched over the *Nunna daul Tsuny* or the Trail Where We Cried back in 1837."

"I've never heard anything so stirring," Silke added as she wiped her eyes with her fingertips.

"I will take you back to the station, this concludes this part of the ceremony. The rest will be out at our sacred burial mound...I will join them after I drop ya'll off," said the venerable Shaman.

"Thank you for inviting us, *Anompoli Lawa*," said Loraine.

"We were happy you could see our ceremony sending the spirit of Red Wolf to his reward, Bone, Loraine, and *Ihoo Kowishto'.*" He nodded at Silke. *"Chihóa-bia-chee,* Red Hair."

"Chihóa-bia-chee, Anompoli Lawa."

As they walked into the station to confirm their return tickets, the telegraph agent approached.

"Telegram for Deputy Bone."

"Here you go." He fished in his pocket and came out with a Morgan silver dollar and handed it to the young agent.

"Wow, thank you sir, will there be a reply?"

"Let me read it first, bub." Bone perused the missive, and then handed it to Silke.

Loraine looked over her shoulder as she read.

"Oh, damn," Silke muttered.

"Reply to Marshal Farmer...On our way...Stop...Meet us at station with our horses...Detective Justice, Loraine, and I will accompany you to Jefferson...Stop...Bone."

§§§

CHAPTER EIGHT

CADDO LAKE

Clay, Maggie, and the others waded across the causeway and ran along the game trail in the direction of the scream.

They stopped abruptly where a hemp rope was hanging down over the trail—its end had been cut by a knife.

Clay knelt down and studied the ground. "Lot's of tracks...Looks like there had been a loop snare in the trail."

"Here's a wire..." started Eli.

"It's a trip wire," interrupted Maggie. "The shiners use these traps to snare game...an' people."

"The shiners have Etta an' Jed?" asked Angel.

Maggie glanced over at her and nodded. "'Fraid so."

"Looks like Etta had stepped in the snare an' Jed was tryin' to get her down when the shiners came in an' got 'em both," commented Clay as he tried to make sense of the myriad tracks.

"Went that way." Maggie pointed. "Southeast...Got a camp 'bout a mile. Place called Taylor Island."

"We have to go get them," exclaimed Daisy.

"Need some help...Only have three guns," said Clay.

"The clan is all armed, I can assure you," commented Maggie.

"But, we can't just leave 'em," cried Daisy.

"I'll slip up on their camp alone an' scout 'em out...They'll never see me unless I want them to," said Maggie.

SILKE'S QUEST

SANTA FE DEPOT
GAINESVILLE, TEXAS

Silke, Bone, and Loraine disembarked the southbound Gulf and Colorado train and saw Marshal Farmer waiting on the platform.

"Your horses, includin' your pack horse, Bart, are down to the hostlers with mine," said Farmer. "East bound leaves in 'bout an hour."

"We appreciate…"

"You didn't think you could go down there without me, did you?" came a voice from behind them.

They turned to see Padrino with Bear Dog at his side, striding up from the livestock pens next to the loading chutes by the tracks.

Bear Dog butted Silke's leg, sat down and put his black paw on her knee.

She knelt and wrapped her arms around his furry neck. "Bear Dog, goodness, seems like you've grown since this mornin'."

He woofed and licked the side of her face.

"Never gave it a thought, Padrino," said Bone.

"Right," the retired Marine replied.

Silke turned to Farmer. "Marshal, why don't you let us take care of findin' those kids? I'm sure gettin' around on that leg in the woods won't be much fun."

"You listen to me, young lady, that's my only son out there and one gimpy leg or no legs at all ain't gonna to keep me from findin' him an' his friends...Don't care if it hairlips the Pope...Are we clear?"

She nodded with a half grin. "Yessir, I do think we are."

JEFFERSON, TEXAS
TEXAS & PACIFIC DEPOT

Silke, Bone, Loraine, Padrino, and Marshal Farmer stepped down the steps from the passenger car. Bear Dog padded alongside Silke as they headed down to the livestock car to unload their horses.

The blue-eyed, black wolf-dog already weighed over eighty pounds and was almost two feet high at the shoulder and wasn't fully grown yet. Every person they passed on the platform gave the group, and especially Bear Dog, ample room.

The railroad hostler had already unloaded all but Bone's seventeen hand, shiny, coal black, half-Friesian gelding. He stepped back up the cleated ramp to the livestock car and led the big horse down to the others.

Bone flipped the young man a silver dollar as he took the lead rope from him. "Appreciate it, son."

"Wow, thank you, sir…He shore is a bigun, but, then again, so 're you…Reckon you needs a horse like him." The colored hostler referred to Bone's 6'8" in height and his 285 pounds.

"Yeah, he suits me fine…Come on Hildebrandt." He led him over to the water trough along with the others already there.

The group let all the horses drink their fill, then tightened up their cinches, mounted and trotted out to the street. They headed toward Jason Murphy's Livery at the edge of town.

They pulled rein outside the wide double doors of the big red livery barn. The owner, in the same worn bib overalls over faded red longjohns, wearing a battered brown fedora, who had taken care of the teenagers, stepped out of the interior.

He spat a viscous stream of tobacco juice onto the scattered hay on the ground. "Howdo, name's Murphy. You be Marshal Farmer, I'm a guessin'," he said as he noticed the City Marshal's badge on his vest.

"Good guess there, old timer…Want to bring us up to date?" Farmer introduced the others.

"Like I said in the telegram, my horses an' mule was astandin' at the corral when I got here this mornin'." He walked over to the corral fence and picked up a rope headstall draped over the top board. "Took this an' others jest like it off'n 'em 'fore I turned 'em in to the corral where they could git to the hay."

Farmer dismounted and took the headstall from Murphy and looked at the end of the lead rope. "Been cut." The marshal glanced back at Bone, and then at the hostler.

"'Zactly…Ever one of 'em…Somebody didn't want the kids leavin', I mind…Jest hope it weren't the shiners."

"Shiners?" asked Padrino.

Murphy filled them in on the moonshiner clan in the swamp.

"That's not good," said Silke.

"No tellin' what a bunch of inbreds might do."

"Can't disagree with that, Marshal," said Bone as he shifted his saddle back to the right to center it on Hildebrandt.

"Any idea where they went?" Silke asked Murphy.

"Nope, jest told 'em to stay to the trails on 'count everthin' looks the same out there."

"Much obliged," said Farmer as he remounted. His bull penis cane was stuck in the rifle boot along with his Winchester.

"I'll see as I can backtrack those horses an' mule. Should be fair easy at least up to when the rain started," commented Silke as she focused on the ground along the trail east…

CADDO LAKE

Maggie studied the shiners camp on Taylor Island from her hide across the narrow waterway. Most were congregated in front of a large clapboard house that had never heard of paint. She watched the activity until it was almost sundown, and then faded away into the shadows of the trees, before she made her way back to Horse Island.

Loraine dropped a double handful of coffee into the pot sitting on a flat rock next to the fire. They had pitched camp alongside Big Cypress Bayou a little over seven miles from Jefferson when it became too dark to follow the tracks.

The stress of the missing teens showed on everyone's face, especially Marshal Farmer's.

Silke noticed him flexing his jaw muscles as he stared into the fire. She moved over and sat beside the veteran lawman and put her hand on his shoulder.

"We'll find them, Marshal…promise."

He glanced over at her. "Got a real bad feelin', Silke…Just can't shake it…God, why did I let 'em go?" Farmer shook his head and looked up at the myriad stars of the Milky Way, twinkling like millions upon millions of tiny campfires overhead.

"I've heard Clay's pretty handy with a gun," said Bone.

The Marshal nodded. "Started teachin' him how to shoot when he was about seven."

"What kind of weapons do they have?" asked Loraine.

Farmer took a breath. "Clay's carryin' his .45 Peacemaker I gave him for graduation...He's as good as I've ever seen with it...Plus, I made 'em take two Winchesters, an '88, an' a '94...Should have made 'em take more."

"Can't figure out who could possibly have wanted to strand 'em in the swamp by cuttin' their horses loose...If they were goin' to steal them, they wouldn't have showed up back to their barn," said Bone.

"No question it was deliberate," commented Padrino.

"Wonder when Maggie's goin' to make it back?" asked Daisy.

"Oh, most anytime now," came a voice from the darkness.

The others turned to see the tall, svelte teen walk into the light made by the campfire.

"We were gettin' worried," said Angel.

"Thanks, but no need...this is my world," Maggie replied. "I smelled coffee...Have any left?"

"Just happen to save you some," replied Clay as he got to his feet, wrapped his deerskin glove around the handle of the hot blue merle graniteware pot, poured her a cup and handed it to her.

She sat down on a log near the fire, blew across the top of her coffee and took a sip.

"Well?" asked Eli.

Maggie looked up, and then around at each one. "Saw 'em...They're in a cage about six feet by six feet made of wooden poles...Just barely room to lie down...Shiners threw a couple pieces of hot water cornbread inside for 'em to eat...Jed picked up one from the dirt floor an' ate it...Etta wouldn't."

"Are they awright?" asked Angel.

Maggie took a deep breath, nodded and finally replied, "So far." She bit her lower lip.

"You think they're gonna do anythin' to 'em?" asked Clay.

"I counted seventeen men an' six women. Some of the men were hangin' 'round the cage laughin' an' talkin' 'bout what they were goin' to do to 'em...startin' with Etta...before they..." She stopped and stared at the coffee in her cup.

"Before they what?" asked Jen.

Maggie's eyes filled as she took several deep breaths, and then looked back up. "Before they..."

§§§

CHAPTER NINE

CADDO LAKE

"Unka Mack, can we go for a walk?" Elizabeth looked up at him.

"Uh, probably not a good idea, honey," said James. "There...uh, have been some bad people nosing around in the last week or so...We'll go outside later and play some croquet...How's that?"

"What kinda bad peoples?"

"Well, they're just swamp people, usually up to no good…and they're just not very nice."

"Can I see one?"

"Uh, probably not, honey, they kinda stay hidden most of the time."James glanced out the window, and then at his brother, Timothy.

The sun was just topping the tall cypress trees as Silke and the group moved away from their camp following the horse's tracks again until they disappeared from the heavy rain the day before.

Bear Dog loped out in front, checking the occasional coon or possum scat. He disappeared around a bend in the game trail that paralleled the bayou.

"Do you think he'll get lost?" asked Loraine.

Silke grinned. "Not likely…He's just explorin'. Checkin' all the new smells." She looked around at the dark, Spanish moss draped woods and black water of the lake on the opposite side from the bayou. "This place is really strange…kinda eerie."

"You could expect one of those ancient dinosaur things to walk up out of that water."

Marshal Farmer watched a large muskrat swimming along the bank.

Suddenly, the water around the animal exploded and churned white as a huge mouth opened under the hapless creature. The muskrat disappeared into the black depths as the water continued to swirl where it had been swimming. The group caught a brief glimpse of a thick scaly tail before the water stilled once more.

"Anybody want to go skinny dippin'?" asked Bone.

"Pass," said Silke.

Bear Dog came trotting back down the trail. It was obvious he was carrying something dark at the front of his mouth with his lips curled back almost in a smile. He stopped at Silke's horse, *Lakna'*, and sat down in the trail.

Silke leaned over and stared at the object he was holding carefully in his front teeth. She dismounted to take a better look.

"What do you have, boy?" She held out her hand.

He dropped the black blob about the size of a marble into it. She looked at it for a moment, mashed it a little between her thumb and forefinger, and then smelled of it.

Silke had a puzzled look on her face as she looked back up at the others. "Smells kind of like licorice…"

"Let me see that, Silke." Marshal Farmer sidled his sorrel gelding over to her and stuck out his hand.

She dropped it in his palm. He looked at it for a moment, and then he too sniffed it, nodded his head, and smiled. "Beeman's Black Jack chewing gum…Clay's favorite."

Silke took the wad of gum back from Farmer, knelt down, put her hand under Bear Dog's chin, looked him in the eyes and held the chewed Black Jack in front of his nose with her other hand. "Find him, Bear Dog, find him."

The black wolf-dog cocked his head for a moment, then turned, and loped back up the trail the way he had come.

"Suggest we follow him." Silke remounted.

"How do you know he has a clue what you said?" asked the marshal.

Silke shook her head. "No idea, he just seems to know what I'm thinking…kinda spooky, actually."

She squeezed her gelding into a trot and followed Bear Dog down the path.

"You think..." Farmer glanced at the others.

"Don't think we ought to argue with her," said Padrino as he bumped Sailor into a trot also.

Farmer, Bone, and Loraine looked at each other, shrugged their shoulders and followed Silke and Padrino along the game trail that bordered the lake.

A set of dark brown eyes watched the group as they made their way through the woods.

"Are you sure that's what you saw, Maggie?" Angel looked at her.

The young girl's skin turned pallid again as she recalled the horrendous sight in the shiner's camp. "No question, I've seen many deer, hogs, and bear carcasses hung from trees an' skinned...It was the same. They were cuttin' away body parts an' puttin' 'em in a big pot."

"Sure they weren't fixin' slop for the hogs?" asked Eli.

Maggie shook her head. "They had already give the skin an' innards to the hogs...'cept for the heart an' liver."

Daisy ran over to the side of the camp and threw up.

"Did you know who it was...I mean was it a man or woman," inquired Clay.

"Man...they cut his sex off an' threw it in the pot, too...Musta been some hunter or fisherman."

Angel joined Daisy and threw up her breakfast also over next to the trees.

"What are ya'll goin' to do?" asked Maggie.

Clay paused and stared at the ground, and then looked up. "Got no choice...We gotta go see if we can get 'em out, before..."

"They're next on the menu," interrupted Eli.

"Etta an' Jed are our friends...Be damned if I'll let them be a bunch of inbred's dinner," said Clay getting to his feet.

"Who would believe there would be cannibals in this day an' time," said Daisy as she walked back up wiping her mouth with a hanky.

"How much ammo we got?" asked Jen.

Clay pursed his lips. "Not enough...got one box of 44-40s for the rifles an' I've got five .45 rounds in my pistol an' twenty-two left in my belt."

"That's it?" Eli arched his eyebrows.

Clay nodded.

"Your dad have any guns or ammo, Maggie?" asked Angel.

She shook her head. "Opposite direction…Take too long to get there an' back."

Bone bumped Hildebrandt up beside Silke and leaned over toward her. "We're bein' watched."

"You see someone?"

He shook his head. "Don't have to…Feel 'em…Dark and malevolent…Pure evil…Dollar to a doughnut it's those shiners old man Murphy was talking about."

"The others know?" Silke asked.

"Not yet. I'll drop back and clue them in…Just wanted you to keep your eyes and ears open…Let's stop for a break first clearing we come to…Got an idea."

Bear Dog stopped in the middle of the trail on the other side of the causeway between the mainland and Horse Island. His blue eyes focused on the teenagers in the camp and watched them intently as they moved about.

"Hey, look over there," said Eli pointing.

"It's a wolf," exclaimed Daisy.

"He's not from around Caddo," commented Maggie.

"How so?" asked Clay.

"I would have seen him before...specially bein' black with blue eyes...He belongs to somebody or he's a spirit wolf."

"Come again?" said Jen.

"The Caddo Indians called them spirit wolves. Weren't around unless they were needed."

"Maybe that's us," commented Angel. "Come here, boy...come on." She whistled and made kissing noises with her lips.

Bear Dog cocked his head first one way, then the other, and then he sat down.

"Maybe he doesn't like water," said Eli.

"No, he's just watchin' us," replied Maggie.

Without warning, Bear Dog's head snapped to the left, he jumped up and ran back down the trail the way he had come.

"Must have gotten tired of watchin'," said Clay.

"I'm goin' to ease back over to the shiner's camp an' see as I can give 'em somethin' else to think about...'sides eatin'."

"You need one of us with a gun to go with you?" asked Clay.

Maggie shook her head. "Nope…Got my knife an' tomahawk, if I need 'em…They're quiet."

"You say so." Clay cocked his right eyebrow.

Maggie jogged over to the causeway, waded across and disappeared into the thick undergrowth and shadows.

"Well, let's check our guns and ammo and make a plan for when Maggie gets back. We're gonna get 'em outta there." Clay pulled his Peacemaker out and checked the rounds.

Silke pulled rein in a small opening where the bayou cut to the south, made a loop, and then went back north. "This looks good to me. Got water on two sides."

"Agreed." Bone dismounted and loosened Hildebrandt's cinch.

Loraine, Marshal Farmer, and Padrino followed suit.

"Anybody for a quick cup of coffee while we let the horses blow?" asked Silke.

"Works for me," said Padrino. "I'll gather up enough deadfall for a hat-sized fire."

Bone handed Hildebrandt's reins to Loraine. "Gonna do a little scouting, babe...Find out who's doggin' us. See that big un here gets him a drink."

"Can do. Be careful, honey."

"Always am."

"Uh-huh, right." She gave him a peck on the lips.

He quietly vanished into the big cathedral-like cypress trees.

Bone moved from tree to tree like a wraith utilizing the skills he learned in the Marine Corps until he spotted a grubby man in dirty blue bib overalls trying to do the same in the direction of Silke and the others. He was downwind from him, sniffed the air and grinned—*moonshine*.

He worked his way to intercept him and just as he was going to step out from behind a thick cottonwood, a black blur flashed from the opposite direction, slamming into the shiner scout.

The skinny, grimy man let out with a partial scream before Bear Dog latched onto his throat and pinned him to the ground.

"Bear Dog…easy, boy…Back off."

The young canine released his hold, glanced up at Bone, and stepped back slightly. His upper lip was lifted in his slight smile.

"Watch him, Bear Dog."

The filthy shiner's eyes got big as saucers as they rolled slightly up at the long white teeth dripping saliva down on his face as they closed to within two inches of his nose.

"Ain't movin' none…Don't let him hurt me," whined Polk, almost without moving his mouth.

"Don't twitch a muscle then, ass-wipe. One word from me…and he'll take your face off…and probably won't stop there."

§§§

CHAPTER TEN

CADDO LAKE

Maggie moved up closer to the bank across the waterway from the moonshiner's enclave and behind a copse of cedar trees.

The women were still tending the cooking pots, adding wild onions and red potatoes.

The body that had hung from a tree by his heels, was gone.

Maggie had gathered some fist-sized rocks on the way over from Horse Island and lobbed one across the water to near the cooking area.

The shiner women at the cook fires jumped, several screamed, at the sound and looked around trying to determine where the rock came from.

Maggie moved about fifteen feet and lobbed another. That one landed at the edge of one of the cook fires, scattering sparks and smaller burning sticks.

She threw one more that bounced from the top of a corrugated   tin shed that the shiners kept dynamite in. They used the high explosive to throw in the water to stun fish.

Maggie giggled as the shiners scattered giving the shed and rock plenty of space, moved back a little deeper into the giant cypress trees and found a limb the size of her arm. Maggie swung it against the hard trunk of one of the trees like a major league baseball player.

The ringing sound resonated through the woods and across the water. It was meant to replicate the 'tree knock' said to be created by the mythical great hairy forest creatures with the big feet, *Sasquatch*.

She did it again.

The men in the camp all picked up their guns and were staring across the waterway into the dense dark woods.

A similar knock sounded from across the lake in answer to Maggie's. She grinned and hit the tree again—once more her knock was answered. She did it one more time for good measure—with the same result, and then faded into the brush back in the direction of the teen's camp...

"Ya'll hear that?" Silke stood to her feet and looked off to the woods on the right.

"Sounds just like the sounds we heard in the Kiamichi Mountains by the *Lofa* creature when we were with the assistant Secretary of the Navy, Teddy Roosevelt," said Loraine. "We call it a *Sasquatch* in our time."

"You saw it?" asked Silke.

Loraine shook her head. "I didn't, but Bone, Bass Reeves, and Mister Roosevelt did. It had a pet panther...They watched the cat kill a three hundred pound black bear, and then said the *Sasquatch* and the panther disappeared into the woods together."

Marshal Farmer looked at Loraine. "Really? You're not funnin' us are you, girl?"

"Sure as I'm sitting here...it happened." She took a sip of her coffee. "Mister Roosevelt said he wouldn't be able to tell a soul...He laughed and flashed that big toothy smile...Then he added, that he 'couldn't get elected dog catcher if he did...The newspapers would all say he was loony, balmy...belongs in the funny farm'."

The knocks sounded two more times, and the woods went eerily quiet.

Polk's eyes got even bigger when he heard the tree knocks.

Bear Dog cocked his head again and looked off across the lake for a moment, and then turned back to the shiner and snarled.

"Don't know which you're the most scared of...that wolf or those knocks from the *Lofa*." Bone knelt down beside Polk and Bear Dog. "But, tell you what, slick...better add me to that list."

Bone pulled his K-Bar from his belt, tested the sharpness with his thumb, and then sucked the small line of blood from it. He placed the edge underneath the shiner's nose.

"Think I could remove your nose and give it to Bear Dog as a treat...Save him havin' to chew it off." Bone paused and thought a second. "But, then again, he just might like to...Decisions, decisions. What to do?"

Polk voided his bladder as his lower lip quivered. His eyes cut from Bear Dog's dripping teeth down to the knife and back again.

"Now, sunshine, I need some information...and you're going to give it to me...aren'tcha?"

Bone could barely hear a muted, "Uh-huh."

He turned as he caught a movement from the corner of his eye.

Maggie stepped out of the shadows. "Who are you?" She noticed Bone's knife under Polk's nose.

"I'm Bone...and you are?"

"Maggie."

"Know anything about a bunch of teenagers out here?"

She nodded. "Gonna kill him?"

"Not yet...Need to know where those kids are...Think he can tell me."

"He can...an' so can I."

Bear Dog turned and looked at Maggie. He cocked his head first one way, and then the other and looked at Bone.

She ruffled the top of his head, he licked her hand, and then returned his attention to Polk.

Ten minutes later, Maggie had brought Bone up to date about the kids and the nature of the shiners.

"Son of a..." He looked down at Polk still under Bear Dog's watchful stare. "Cannibals?" Bone shook his head. "Worthless scum suckin'..."

He brought his knife back down to the man's nose.

"Wait." Maggie put her hand on his arm. "Might could use him."

Bone frowned. "How so?"

"There's no way for us to get across to their island without bein' seen." Maggie glanced down at Polk. "But, this one can..."

"Ah...Damn...got it. That's good girl."

He looked back down at the shiner. "Now here's what you're going to do, you slimy chunk of gator crap...and if you don't..." He leaned closer to the odoriferous swamp man. "I'll send this wolf to find you and rip your face off...You won't know when he's coming an' you damn sure won't see him...but come...he will...Comprendo?"

An hour later, Bone, Maggie, and Bear Dog walked out of the woods into Marshal Farmer's camp. Everyone jumped as they seemed to just materialize out of the shadows.

"Damn you, Bone, could have given us some warning." Loraine whacked him across his broad chest.

"Sorry, babe, didn't think about it...Hey, this is Maggie. She knows where the kids are...an' ya'll ain't gonna believe this, but..."

Ten minutes later he had filled them in—they tightened up their cinches, mounted, and followed Maggie and Bear Dog down the narrow game trail.

When they arrived at the causeway across from Horse Island. Maggie turned to Bone and the others.

"Gonna go back to Taylor Island an' lead Jed an' Etta back here soon's that shiner gets them cut loose."

"Think he'll be able to do it?" Marshal Farmer looked at her.

"If you'd a seen how scared he was of Bone an' Bear Dog you wouldn't have to ask."

"How's he going to do it?" asked Loraine.

"Probably wait till sundown an' after they eat what they been cookin' up all day 'fore he cuts the rope holdin' the door on their cage."

Loraine and Silke both shook like wet dogs and gagged.

Padrino nudged Sailor forward. "How deep is the waterway between the island and the mainland?"

"Little over waist deep an' 'bout twenty yards."

"What about the gators?" asked Farmer.

Maggie pursed her lips. "Chance they gotta take...Hope they know to swim an' not try to wade...Makes too much racket."

"Let's hope so," said Silke.

"What if the shiners hear them?" offered Bone.

Maggie grinned. "Gonna give 'em somethin' else to think about again…" She looked at Silke. "Can you tell Bear Dog to come with me?"

Silke smiled and nodded. "Go with her, boy."

He spun around twice and sat down beside Maggie.

"He likes you," Silke said.

"Uh-huh…Like him too."

She and Bear Dog disappeared back into the undergrowth.

Silke shook her head. "Move like ghosts."

They nudged their horses across the causeway and up the bank of Horse Island.

Clay and the others ran up to them.

"Dad! How did ya'll find us?" Clay took his father's reins as the elder Farmer dismounted and pulled his cane from his rifle boot.

They hugged.

"Maggie led us," commented Bone.

Daisy took the reins for Loraine's Sweet Face mare, and Bone's gelding, Hildebrandt. "She's amazin'. Really knows her way around this swamp."

"Ya'll got'ny coffee?" asked Silke.

"Just happen to have some," responded Eli.

Angel took Silke's reins as she dismounted, too. "Fixin' to put some catfish we caught this afternoon on to fry…Ya'll hungry?"

"Thought you'd never ask, Little Bit." Bone unbuckled his saddlebags and bedroll.

Clay looked down at the ground. "Uh…Guess Maggie told ya'll 'bout Etta an' Jed?"

Padrino grinned. "Bone convinced one of those inbreds it would be in his best long term interest to arrange for them to escape tonight…Maggie an' Bear Dog went back to lead them here."

Angel looked puzzled. "Bear Dog?"

Bone grinned. "Silke's wolf."

Clay, Daisy, Angel, Jen, and Eli all responded simultaneously, "Wolf?"

"Oh," exclaimed Angel. "Black, blue eyes…He was watchin' us earlier."

§§§

CHAPTER ELEVEN

CADDO LAKE

Maggie picked up a limb to use as a bat to knock on the cypress trees again before she reached the shiner's island.

She slipped through the brush up behind the same copse of cedar trees she had hidden behind

Ken Farmer

before to spy on the island. Bear Dog crawled on his belly beside her.

It was just past gloaming and the creeping shadows were creating eerie patterns across the waterway. They mingled with the passing shadows caused by the three quarter gibbous moon as scattered high clouds occasionally passed across its face.

Maggie could see the wooden cage was empty by the flickering blazes on the other side. She searched the near bank for signs of the two teens—nothing. Then she caught movement at the edge of the water.

A shadowy form slipped out from behind a tree and into the black lake next to the shiner's four pirogues pulled up on the bank, and started silently swimming the twenty yards to the mainland.

Maggie swung the thick limb against the bole of one of the trees, creating the resonant ring of a 'tree knock'.

As before, the men scurried about, grabbed their long guns and backed toward their fires forming a protective circle. They tried to peer into the darkness outside the camp, but their night vision had been destroyed by looking at their bright fires.

She hit the tree again, and as earlier, there was an answering knock, but this time, it was closer.

Maggie moved down to the water's edge to help the swimmer up the slick bank. She reached out to grab an arm and pulled Etta out of the lake and quickly into the brush.

"Where's Jed?"

Etta fell into Maggie's arms, sobbing.

"Where's Jed?" she repeated.

"Oh, God, Maggie…they…they…took him." Her body shook with violent sobs as she tried to catch her breath. "He's…he's hangin' in that big tree at the edge…edge of camp…They…Oh, sweet Jesus…they…"

"Awright, Etta…I understand…There's nothin' we can do now. Come on, let's get out of here."

One of the men in the camp noticed the cage was empty. "Big Daddy, she's gone!"

There were fifteen men and seven women in the moonshiner's enclave—over half were Big Daddy's offspring from his own daughters.

The patriarch of the shiners, Zeke, Big Daddy, Carter, a big bellied, dark bearded, churlish man, spat a long stream of thick, pungent, tobacco juice to the bare ground beside his worn Jefferson brogans. "Damn you, Cobb, you's 'posed to be watchin' her."

Cobb, the oldest of the Carter children, had rushed over to the cage. "Looky here, rope's cut. How'd she do that? Skinny bitch didn't have no knife."

He turned to Polk. "You fed 'em 'fore we hung the boy in that tree to bleed out…You knock yerself off a little nooky an' let her steal yer knife?…That it?"

Big Daddy approached Polk and grabbed him by the front of his overalls. "You listen to me, you worthless whelp of a whore, you go find her…er by God you'll be a takin' her place…Got that?"

He shook the skinny man like a rag doll and shoved him to the ground. "Now git."

"But, Big Daddy…"

"Git," Carter roared.

Polk disappeared into the darkness in the direction of the mainland.

Maggie led a still distraught Etta through the woods toward Horse Island. Bear Dog padded along beside them.

Abruptly the young wolf-dog stopped and turned around. A low growl rumbled from his throat as the hair along his back stood up. He peered intently with his blue eyes back the way they had come.

"What is it, boy, they on our tail?" Maggie knelt down beside him, and also looked back into the darkness.

She rose back up and again took Etta by the hand. "Let's keep movin'."

The night sounds of frogs, birds, and insects of the swampy woodlands suddenly went silent, and then the quiet was shattered by a long, high-pitched scream that ended with a gurgling sound.

Maggie and Etta exchanged glances and picked up their pace.

Bear Dog remained in the middle of the trail, staring back into the darkness in the direction of the weird scream. His lips were curled up into a snarl and a low guttural growl continued from his throat for a moment before he turned and trotted after the two girls.

125

"My God, what was that?" Loraine shot to her feet from her place beside the camp fire. She looked over at Bone.

He shook his head. "Wasn't no panther, I can tell you that."

"Sounded like a man," offered Padrino.

Marshal Farmer looked off into the blackness. "Heard a scream like that when I was in the cavalry durin' the Injun wars in Arizona." He looked at the others. "One of our men was caught by the Apache…They have very painful ways of killin' a man…Ain't pretty, neither."

Bone stood, pulled his Smith & Wesson 500, .50 caliber hand gun and checked the loads. "Going to see if Maggie and the kids are headed this way."

"I'll go with you." Silke pitched the remains of her coffee in the fire where it sizzled and popped on a burning log.

"Not necessary, Silke, this is what I do."

"Not askin' your permission, Bone."

An enigmatic grin spread across his face as he nodded, raised his eyebrows, and turned toward the causeway. "Put it that way, girl, let's go."

Silke quickly checked her own 500, plus loosened her warhawk in her beaded belt and followed him out of the campfire illuminated area into the pale moonlight.

They waded across the causeway and melted into the shadows of the heavy growths of Spanish moss hanging from the cypress and oak trees like daphanous lace gowns.

The 6'8" Bone moved like a phantom through the mottled darkness—but no less so was Silke, right behind him.

"How do you know where you're goin'?"

Bone turned his head slightly. "Don't...Just follow my instincts...Think like a predator."

"Like that." Silke grinned and nodded.

After thirty minutes, Bone held up his hand, but Silke almost bumped into his back anyway.

"Listen," he said sotto voce.

"I hear 'em," she whispered back.

Silke felt a nudge against her tall Apache moccasin clad leg. "Bear Dog." She knelt down and put her arm about the neck of the almost invisible animal.

"Maggie, it's us," he said softly.

The muted silhouettes of her and Etta materialized from up the trail.

"Oh, Mister Bone." Etta threw her arms about his thick neck and nestled her face in his chest.

"Where's Jed?" he asked, but he could see Maggie behind her shake her head, her long red pony tail swung back and forth—the highlights glinted in the pale moon.

He nodded. "Take her on into camp…going to check ya'll's back trail."

"We heard a scream…"

Bone interrupted Maggie, "We heard it, too." He headed on the way they had come.

"We'll take Bear Dog. It's clear back to the island." Silke hurried to catch up with the big man while Bear Dog went on ahead of them both.

A half-mile further on, they could see the flickering fire lights in the distance from the shiner's camp through the trees.

Again Bone stopped in the trail. A body lay crumpled at his feet.

He knelt down. "One of the shiners…Same one we caught before…Deader'n hell."

Bear Dog stared into the shadowy darkness to the right. A low growl rumbled from his throat.

Bone pulled out his small tactical *LED* light from his time, hooded the lens with his hand and shined it on Polk's face.

"My God," whispered Silke. "What happened to him? Look at the blood coming from his mouth, nose, and ears."

Bone lifted one of Polk's eyelids. "Petechial hemorrhage."

"What's that?"

"See the bloodshot eyes?"

"So, what does that mean?"

"The tiny blood vessels called capillaries in the eyes burst."

"How?"

"He was suffocated."

Bone felt of the man's ribs. "Damn…most of his ribs are broken." He looked up at her. "Our good buddy here was crushed to death." He pointed down at the ground beside the body with his light. "Look at the size of those tracks."

"But…"

"Come on." He rose and headed toward the flickering lights.

Silke and Bear Dog followed right behind him.

They peered through the foliage at the shiner's camp. They could see everyone huddled about the fires, casting occasional fearful glances into the darkness on the mainland.

"They're scared," said Bone.

"Why?" Silke cut her eyes at him.

"What do you think?"

"They know what it was that killed Polk?"

He nodded. "I'd say."

"They're going to think the *Sasquatch* is the Easter Bunny when I'm through. They'll never do to anyone else what they've done to Jed."

"What's the Easter Bunny?"

Bone glanced at her and smiled. "Somewhere about the 1700s, German immigrants in Pennsylvania brought their tradition of an egg-laying rabbit called *Osterhase*. The children would make nests in which this creature could lay colored eggs...In our time, we call him the Easter

Bunny, and we hide colored eggs all over for the kids to find."

"Oh, how fun."

"The Easter Bunny is a big lovable creature…but ain't going to be anything like what we're going to do." He looked back at the camp. "Wonder what that tin shed is? Doesn't look like a privy."

"Ask Maggie, bet she knows."

Bone nodded.

They exchanged steely-eyed stares with the moonlight glinting from the black water between them and the cannibal's camp.

Silke flexed her jaw muscles. "They best check their souls to God…because their asses belong to us."

Bone and Silke bumped fists.

§§§

CHAPTER TWELVE

CADDO LAKE

"It got 'im, Big Daddy…it got 'im." Marvin stared into the moonlit darkness across the waterway shaking like a wet mule.

"Heard, stupid." The rotund leader looked around, not sure what to say or do next.

He cut a big chunk from his twist of Brown's Mule Chewing Tobacco with his skinning knife.

"What now, Big Daddy?" Cobb nervously glanced across the water.

"Shut up, fool, I'm thinkin'." He shoved the tobacco into the side of his mouth and started wallowing it around with his tongue. "Awright, here's what...Cobb..." He spat a stream of the viscous amber fluid off to the side. "...take Marvin, Chesley, an' Rooster, a couple pirogues an'...

"What was that, Unka James?...Sounded like someone screamin' outside somewhere a long ways off." Elizabeth tried to look out a window at the moonlight glinting from the still, mirror-like, surface of the lake water.

"Oh, some kind of animal, honey." He added another log to the blaze in the rock fireplace. "Hungry?"

"Uh-huh."

"The stew's about ready. Want to give me a hand, brother?" He glanced over at Timothy on the leather couch.

"Of course…That sourdough bread you baked smells great, too."

"Had the starter I got from mama twenty years ago…Still good."

"What happened to grandmother, Unka Mack?"

"She got sick, baby. It's called the consumption. People that have it can't breathe very well and cough a lot."

A sad look came over the young girl's face as her lower lip protruded slightly. "That's so sad."

"She had to move to Santa Fe, New Mexico. The air is a lot dryer there and better for her lungs."

Timothy got to his feet and held out his hand to Elizabeth. "And she's doing some better…Got a letter from her last month."

They walked across the room to the oak plank table where James had started setting bowls of venison stew with thick slices of steaming sourdough bread and a big jar of wild honey in front of their chairs.

"Can we go visit her sometimes?…Haven't seen her since I was little."

Timothy pulled out a chair for Elizabeth to sit down, and then pushed her back up close to the table. There were several large books in the seat to raise her up to the table top.

"Think that might be a wonderful idea, honey...Maybe we'll catch a train west in a couple of weeks." Timothy glanced at James.

"Sounds good, brother...maybe I'll come with ya'll."

Timothy poured Elizabeth a glass of buttermilk, and then put the pitcher back in the in-ground cooler under a small trap door in the floor of the kitchen.

He came back and took his seat next to her and spread his napkin in his lap.

"This is really good, Unka James." Elizabeth dabbed her mouth after eating a spoonful of the rich stew.

"Why, thank you, Elizabeth." James turned his head in the direction of the barn outside.

"What is it?" asked Timothy.

"Horses are bothered by something...Hear 'em?"

Timothy listened and could hear the horses snort and stomp their feet out in their stalls. "Coon or possum?"

James shook his head. "Uh-uh. They're used to them...This is something else."

Timothy got to his feet, walked to the door and lifted his brother's double barreled Remington twelve gauge from its rack over the header. He broke it over, checked the loads and snapped it back closed.

"I'll go check...just relax, brother, you cooked supper."

"Probably a catamount or bobcat prowling about. Just you coming out of the house will probably scare him off."

Tim closed the thick plank door behind him.

James cocked his head trying to listen for any aberrant sounds from outside. Hearing nothing, he strode over to the pegs in the log wall next to the door and pulled Timothy's 7.62 caliber Nagant pistol from its holster.

"Is Unka Mack all right?"

"Oh, I think so, honey. He'll be back in..."

The still night was shattered by a loud blast from the shotgun, followed immediately by the sound of several rifle shots. There was one more explosion from the 12 gauge, and then silence...

Silke, Bone, and Bear Dog crossed the causeway and strode into the camp. Etta was wrapped in a blanket next to the fire, nursing on a cup of coffee.

Loraine, Padrino, Marshal Farmer, and the teens looked up as the trio entered into the zone of firelight.

Bear Dog promptly laid down close to the campfire.

Loraine poured cups of coffee for Silke and Bone as they walked up to the fire. "Find out what that scream was?" She handed each a steaming cup.

"Thanks, babe." He squatted down, blew across the top, licked the rim, and took a sip, and then nodded. "Oh, yeah...One of the shiners...He had been squashed...most of his bones broken."

"Do what?" Marshal Farmer looked up from his cup. "What do you mean, 'squashed'?"

"Just that. Looked like he'd been run over by a herd of horses."

"But how?" asked Loraine.

Bone looked at his wife. "*Lofa, Sasquatch*, Big Foot, hairy man of the forest...whatever you want to call him...Crushed the shiner like a ripe plum."

Ken Farmer

"Why?" Daisy furrowed her brow and looked at Bone.

"Pissed the big guy off is my guess...I can tell you this, though...Those inbred bastards are scared to death of him."

Maggie smiled as she sipped on her coffee. "That's why I knocked on the trees...It's how they communicate with each other...I called him."

"Wasn't that kinda dangerous?" questioned Clay.

Maggie shook her head. "They've never bothered me, but there must be some kind of war goin' on 'tween them an' the shiners...Think they killed one of the juveniles of what you're callin' *Sasquatchs* back a few years ago."

Padrino nodded. "That would tend to do it, I would think...They apparently have a family type structure...Don't mess with the kids."

They looked up at the sound of two knocks that echoed from the mainland. Maggie quickly got to her feet, grabbed a large branch from the firewood pile and whacked a cypress at the edge of the camp one time, and then came back to the fire.

Bear Dog raised up on his front feet, stuck his nose up in the direction of the three-quarter moon and let go with a long mournful howl, and then promptly laid back down.

Bone shrugged his big shoulders while the others exchanged glances.

James cautiously opened the door and quickly stepped outside. He turned back to close it.

"Lock this behind me and don't open it unless it's me or Uncle Mack...Understand?"

Elizabeth nodded. "Uh-huh."

He closed it and listened for her to throw the large dead bolt on the inside, and then he moved silently toward the barn. He cocked his revolver.

There was enough light from the moon that he could make out most things next to the barn and over to the water. James could see two forms lying on the ground near the dock where he kept his pirogue.

He eased over and knelt down beside the body nearest the barn—it was Timothy...

"Damn fools, cain't count on you to do nothin' right." Cobb reached forward and slapped Rooster against the side of his head. "Got our brother, Chesley, kilt...Dumb bastard."

Rooster turned and looked back at Cobb paddling on the back seat. "Couldn't hep it...How wuz I to know he wuz acarryin' a scattergun?"

Marvin leaned over and popped Rooster across the back with his paddle from the other pirogue alongside Cobb and Rooster's as they paddled back across the black lake. "You know Big Daddy wuz partial to Chesley on account of him bein' a mite slow."

Cobb nodded. "Yeah...Big Daddy may hang you in the tree 'stead of that pilgrim...You know he wuz countin' on us."

"Wadn't my fault Chesley come arunnin' at him with jest a stick...Shot quick as I could...Hit 'im twicet, I think."

"Ya'll shoulda drug his body to the boats 'fore the other one come out." Cobb angrily dug his paddle deep to send the jon boat skimming across the glass slick surface.

Night fog was forming on the surface of the lake making it even more eerie.

"I wuz shot…Who's gonna dig these pellets outta my ass he planted there when he wuz a fallin'? Huh?…Tell me that?" Marvin whined.

"Mama'll dig 'em out with her scalin' knife…" muttered Cobb. "Big Daddy wuz a wantin' that little girl fer his ownself."

Maggie looked off to the east at the sound of the gunfire with concern on her face. "That sounds like it could have come from our cabin."

Silke turned to her. "How far is ya'll's cabin?"

"Mile an' a half…er two, I mind. It's at the end of that bayou over there." She pointed.

Bone peered into the darkness. "Sounded like a firefight…Shotgun and rifle."

§§§

CHAPTER THIRTEEN

CADDO LAKE

James picked up his brother's limp body in his arms and carried him back to the cabin. He knocked on the door with the toe of his boot.

"Elizabeth, it's Uncle James. Let me in, honey."

A short moment later, he heard the steel bolt being slid back with a thunk, and the door opened inward. Elizabeth peeked around the edge.

"Unka Mack!…Is he…"

James turned sideways to get through the doorway with his brother in his arms. "Not yet, honey, but he's hurt awful bad…Run get me some towels and we need to get some water on the stove to boil."

"Oh, oh…Yes, Unka James." She spun on her heel, tears already running down her cheeks as she ran to the linen cabinet to get the towels.

James laid Timothy on his bed and removed his shirt. He looked down at the two bloody holes, one in the upper left chest and the other in the lower right—small frothy bubbles were forming in the blood from the bottom wound.

"Damn."

Elizabeth ran into the bedroom with a stack of towels.

"Need the water, baby. Is it hot yet?"

"Almost, Unka James. I'll go check it again."

"Be careful, don't burn yourself."

"I won't."

She ran back out of the room to the kitchen.

James ripped one of the towels in half and folded each into a pad. He rolled his brother a little to the side, saw the exit wound in his upper back, just above his shoulder blade, placed one pad over it and lowered him back down.

There was no exit wound for the bottom bullet.

He pressed the second pad on the top entry wound, tore another towel in two, cleaned most of the blood away from the lower one, and then placed a pad over it. James held pressure on both wounds with his hands.

Tim's eyes fluttered, and then opened. He looked up at James. "Hit bad, brother?"

"Never seen anyone that was hit good with a bullet...but if I can get the bleeding stopped..."

"Hard to breathe." Timothy tried to take a deeper breath and winced at the additional sharp pain.

"Breathe easy, Tim, breathe easy. The lower bullet clipped your lung a little and broke a couple ribs...seen worse."

"You're just...just full of good news, aren't you?"

"Not going to blow smoke on you, brother. It ain't good...It was the shiners, wasn't it?"

Timothy nodded, squeezed his eyes and pursed his lips against the burning pain. "Yeah…ugly, nasty bastards." He looked up again. "What do you they want?"

James furrowed his brow. "Us."

The night fog rolled into the teen's camp from the lake side. It was so thick they couldn't see all the way across the clearing and the glow from the fire only penetrated eight or nine feet.

"Funny how fog deadens sounds…can't even hear the horses chompin' grass or snufflin' anymore." Silke cocked her head trying to listen.

"We always put out extra guards over in Afghanistan on the rare occasions we had fog. Ragheads liked to try to infiltrate our perimeter." Bone took a long sip of his coffee.

"The gooks did the same in 'Nam…Sometimes we found two or three of our patrol with their throats cut come morning…'Course that gate swung both ways," added Padrino.

Marshal Farmer glanced at the others. "Santa Anna had his band play the song *El Degüello* at the siege of the Alamo."

Silke cocked her right eyebrow. "What does *El Degüello* mean?"

Loraine looked over at her. "It's Spanish for, *slit throat* or *throat cutting* where there was to be no-quarter given to the enemy."

"It's been said that the band started playing it the morning of March 6, 1836, as the final assault began, and they continued until the Alamo fell…They executed the four or five survivors…some say included Davy Crockett, but others, that his body was found surrounded by the corpses of no less than sixteen Mexican soldiers…Santa Anna then had all the Texian's bodies piled up an' burnt. The women and a slave were released," commented Padrino.

Bone got to his feet. "Think I see what you're sayin', Marshal…Need to pay those inbreds a little visit."

Silke followed suit and Bear Dog raised up also. "Let's go." She checked her 500 again.

"Believe I'll tag along. Been a while since I've done this…but you don't forget how…Had a necklace I made in 'Nam…Wouldn't let me bring it back, though," said Padrino.

"What kind of necklace?" asked Silke.

Padrino's eyes flashed in the firelight. "Ears."

"Oooh...gag," said Daisy and Angel together.

Padrino licked his fingers, reached over to the edge of the fire, rubbed them in the ashes, and then spread them over both cheeks, nose, and his forehead.

"What's that for?" asked Silke.

"Keeps any light from bouncing from my shiny white face."

"Interestin'." She cocked her head and imitated his actions, as did Bone.

"We carried sticks of two colors of grease paint over in the desert...Even the black guys used it because the oil in their skin would reflect light. These ashes should work fine...'specially in the fog...Let's move out."

Maggie stood to her feet also. "Want me to guide you, Bone?"

"No, honey, know how to get there now. Thanks...You and Marshal Farmer keep an eye on things here...We'll go check your cabin in the morning."

She nodded. "Thank you."

Cobb, Marvin, and Rooster walked hangdogged into the shiner's camp.

Big Daddy jumped to his feet when they stepped from the dense fog into the small circle of firelight. "Where's Chesley?...An' where's the pilgrims?"

Cobb shuffled his feet and looked at the ground. "Uh...Well, you see...Big Daddy...it's...uh..."

"Damn you all to hell...You got yer brother kilt...didn'tcha?...Usless as tits on a..." He stomped a tight circle, stopped and looked at his three offspring in the murky light.

"One of them guys, he come...come outside ashootin' a big scattergun...Chesley run at him with just a stick 'fore I could stop him an' got blowed all to hell, he did," Rooster spat out while he had the chance. "I put a couple rounds in the guy...I think."

Big Daddy whirled on Rooster. "You think?...Since when?...Chesley was just 'sposed to hep carry the bodies...Dammit to hell."

He stomped another circle, and then whirled back around. "Ya'll git yer asses back in them boats an' go git yer brother's body." He turned to the group of shiners watching. "Coot an' Wash, ya'll go 'cross to the mainland, find whatever's left of Polk an' bring him back…Waste not, want not."

Silke, Bone, Padrino, and Bear Dog crossed the causeway and worked their way silently through the pea soup fog into the woods.

"Bear Dog, go." Silke pointed in the direction of the shiner's island.

The nearly invisible black wolf-dog moved ahead of Bone and led the way through brush.

Bone shook his head. "Dang, he's smart. He's keeping just in sight…not six feet ahead of us." He looked back at Silke right behind him.

"How does he know to do that?"

"Told him to."

"Huh?"

"He knows what she's thinking, Bone," offered Padrino.

"Oh, right…Knew that." Bone ducked a limb across the trail.

Silke grinned and also ducked. "Uh-huh."

Padrino didn't.

"Ow…Ya'll could say something."

"Will next time…If we remember," commented Silke.

"Thanks…Don't do me any favors."

"Hope we don't run into any of Maggie's hairy friends tonight," said Bone.

"Only fools and drunks would be traipsing through a swamp in a fog like this."

Silke glanced over her shoulder. "Which are we, Padrino?"

"Bone didn't bring any tequila, so you figure it out."

"Point."

Bone held up his hand—they stopped. Bear Dog stood in the trail, the hair along his back was up and a low growl rumbled from his throat.

He turned back to Silke and Padrino and spoke sotto voce. "Think there's a couple shiners up the trail gathering what's left of Polk." Bone grinned. "Listen, here's what we're gonna do…

Coot and Wash crept along the trail, feeling the ground with their feet. They each carried their hunting rifles.

"What if that thang's still here?" Wash whispered.

"Mind he's long gone by now," answered Coot.

"Think?"

"Do."

"What if it ain't?" asked Wash.

"How fast kin you run?" Coot's foot nudged against Polk's body still in the trail. "Found 'im...Found 'im."

He knelt down and felt of the body. "Dang...Feels like a sack of sweet taters...lumpy, like all busted up."

Twenty-five feet up the trail a huge form, backlit by a strange light, raised both long arms above its head and roared like all the banshees in hell.

"Oh, God, it's him...Run Coot," screamed Wash as he turned, fell down, got back up, his feet slipping on the damp moss on the ground.

He lost his footing again, did a header, managed to get back up and ran stumbling down the trail to the lake.

Coot stumbled over Polk's body, but rolled over when he hit the ground and pulled the trigger of the old Civil War era Spencer .52 caliber carbine he was carrying at the shadowy creature.

A massive blinding flash and explosion from the old big bore rifle was immediately followed by another roar from the figure as the shiner dropped the rifle, scrambled to his feet and followed Wash back down the trail, screaming as he ran…

§§§

CHAPTER FOURTEEN

CADDO LAKE

"Uh-oh." Loraine's head snapped around as she stared off into the fog in the direction Bone and the others went. "That's wasn't Bone or Silke's .50 cal...That was a big bore rifle."

"Shiners got some Spencers an' Sharps. Heard 'em before," said Maggie.

Marshal Farmer got to his feet and cocked his head to listen to the quiet of the fogbound lake. "Gonna say sounded like a Spencer…Some of us had 'em an' some had Springfields in the cavalry…Either would get it done…'Nybody hear 'nythin' else?"

"Sound doesn't carry very well in fog, but thought I heard a cry or yell," said Loraine.

Bone dropped to his knees in the trail with his head almost touching the ground.

Silke ran up to him and knelt down. "Bone! Bone! Are you hit?"

His body shook as he raised his head, tears of laughter were running down his face as he tried to catch his breath. "Funniest thing I've ever seen." He giggled and rose to his feet.

"Damn you, Bone, thought you were shot." Silke whacked him across the back.

A huge grin spread across his face. "No, no…Look." He shined his TAC light across Polk's body to the Spencer the shiner had dropped after pulling the trigger.

Padrino walked over and picked up the carbine. "Well, son of a gun...It blew up."

He showed Silke the split barrel, and then turned the rifle around and looked at the muzzle and grinned. "Full of mud."

"Must have jammed it in the ground when he tripped over Polk's body." Silke leaned over and studied the dirt next to the body. "Yep, right here." She pointed to a gouge in the trail.

Bear Dog walked stiff-legged up to the body and sniffed of it.

Silke turned to Bone. "How did you know what those things sounded like?"

He grinned. "We had one of those TV shows I told you about in our time...It was called *Finding Bigfoot*, and they're always out in the boonies at night trying to find one...They had a recording of what was supposed to be one and one or more of the hosts would imitate it to try to call one of the creatures up so they could take a picture of it."

"So that's why you had Padrino shine his light stick thing on your back from down low..."

"Uh-huh...Made me be nothing but a big shadow...now not as big as one of the *Sasquatches*, but at twenty feet in the darkness...they couldn't tell." Bone giggled again. "Has to be one of the best gags I've ever pulled...Bet they both peed their pants."

Padrino nodded. "Pretty close, I'd say, Bone."

Bone leaned down over Polk's body, untied the rope he had around his waist for a belt and held it up to his light.

"Those shiners will send somebody back in the daylight to see about the body." Bone glanced at Silke and Padrino. "Gonna hang it in the middle of the trail from a branch by one foot."

Silke laughed. "That oughta add to it. They won't expect one of those creatures can tie a knot in a rope."

"Uh-huh...right on, Silke."

"Right on where?"

It was Padrino's turn to chuckle. "It's an expression from our time meaning you hit the nail on the head."

"Then why don't ya'll just say that?"

Padrino started to answer but was interrupted by a muted guttural cry similar to Bone's from a short distance away.

They exchanged glances.

"Guess that calling works just like knocking on trees does."

"I'd say so, Silke...We best get a hurry on." Bone grabbed one of Polk's feet, tied the rope around the ankle and held him up off the ground with the leg close to a limb. "Tie him off, Padrino."

The retired Master Gunnery Sergeant quickly knotted the other end of the rope around the branch, leaving Polk's body swinging above the trail.   "Done."

"Now, let's make like a cow patty and hit the trail."

Bone led off back the way they came with Bear Dog padding along side.

"You know, Bone, sometimes I don't have any idea what ya'll are sayin'."

Padrino chuckled again. "Don't feel like the Lone Ranger, Silke, sometimes I don't either."

"Who?"

Twenty minutes later, the trio and Bear Dog entered the camp from out of the fog.

Loraine rushed up and hugged Bone, and then kissed him.

"Wow, I may have to leave more often."

"You do, you big lug, and I'll hurt you." She stepped back and hit him on one of his broad shoulders. "What happened? Who fired that shot?…We heard what sounded like two screams…"

"Whoa, whoa…chill out, babe…Let me have a cup of coffee and we'll bring you up to snuff." He had his patented grin across his face.

"Yes, dear." Loraine pecked him on the lips and poured him a cup of coffee. "Better make it good."

Silke and Padrino fetched their own cups and took seats on a big log next to the fire.

Fifteen minutes later they had filled everyone in on their scouting excursion with Bone doing most of the telling and giggling all the while.

Bone leaned back against the log, took a last sip of his coffee, and pitched the grounds into the fire.

"And that's pretty much it...Those inbreds apparently have a morbid fear of those creatures."

Marshal Farmer removed his hat and wiped the sweatband with his kerchief. "So that second scream was from one of them?"

Bone, Padrino, and Silke collectively raised their eyebrows.

"Ah...I see."

Silke looked over at Maggie. "Have you ever seen one?"

The svelte teen shrugged her shoulders. "No, just seen tracks an' their leavin's."

"What do you mean, leavin's?" asked Loraine.

"I tol' Clay an' them earlier 'bout findin' a bunch of tracks, adult an' young where they were eatin' clams...They threw these away."

Maggie opened her possibles pouch and took out a handful of blue and wine pearls. She gave one each to Bone, Farmer, Silke, Loraine, and Padrino.

Marshal Farmer sat up and leaned toward the fire to take a better look at the blue one she gave him. "Great guns..." He glanced over at Maggie, and then at Silke. "Blue fresh water pearls."

Loraine looked at hers. "Mine's wine colored."

"Mine too," added Silke.

Maggie grinned. "Blue for boys and wine for the ladies."

Bone mumbled a short clip of a Toby Keith song, "Whisky for my men an' beer for my horses."

Silke furrowed her brow. "Do what?"

"Nothing."

Padrino rolled his pearl back and forth between his thumb and forefinger, holding it up to the firelight. "Flawless." He looked over at Maggie. "You have any idea what these are worth?"

She shrugged her shoulders. "Don't need 'em. There's a lots more where they were eatin' those clams...just layin' 'round with the smashed shells...on the other side of the lake." Maggie pointed east.

Silke glanced at hers again. It was almost a half-inch in diameter. She looked around at the others, and then noticed Etta, still wrapped in the blanket—she was sitting on the far end of the log, staring at the ground, not listening to any of the conversations.

Silke got to her feet, moved over and sat down beside her. It was evident she hadn't said a word since she and Bone intercepted her and Maggie after her escape. Bear Dog was lying next to her, his head was resting on one of her feet.

She took Etta's hand and helped her to her feet. "Etta, let's go over to one of the tents. Would you like to talk?"

Her green-eyed, tear-streaked face looked up at Silke. She pursed her lips and made an almost imperceptible nod with her head.

Silke led her over to Clay's tent and opened the front flap. As soon as they were inside, Etta turned, wrapped her arms around Silke and the flood gates opened.

Her body shook with hard sobs as she tried to breathe between them. She tried to speak, but no words would come. Silke could feel the wetness of Etta's tears on her own cheeks. There was nothing she could do except to hold the devastated girl and let her cry it out.

Several times Etta tried to talk, but to no avail. Her body continued to shake.

Silke lowered them both to the tent floor and could only hold her tight and whisper, "Let it go, Etta, let it all go...I'm here for you." Her own salty tears mingled with Etta's, and she realized she couldn't speak anymore either.

The two girls cried together for what seemed to Silke to be hours, but she knew it was only fifteen minutes or so.

Finally Etta leaned her head back. "Oh, Silke, it was horrible, so horrible..." Tears started running afresh. "I couldn't do anything to help him."

She looked deep into Silke's sky blue eyes. "He was my friend, Silke...Known Jed since we were little." Her body racked again. She snuffled. "They stripped him naked an' the men...the men...did things to him...Oh, God..." She buried her face in Silke's shoulder.

"I know, honey, I know." Silke put her hand behind Etta's head and cried along with her.

Etta took a big breath and leaned back again. "Then when they were through...they...they hung him upside down in that tree...an'...an' then...then...they cut his..."

"I know...I know...There was nothing you could do."

"Silke...the animals...gutted...gutted him like like a...a hog." She took another breath and sobbed out, "Filthy, filthy...animals."

"They'll pay, honey...I promise you that. They'll pay."

Etta looked at her again. "If ya'll hadn't captured Polk an'…an' made him open the cage door…Oh, God…Oh, God…" She shook like a leaf. "Oh, God, Silke…I…I was next."

§§§

CHAPTER FIFTEEN

MCPHERSON CABIN

"Is Elizabeth in…in bed?" wheezed Timothy as he squeezed his eyes against the pain.

James wiped his brother's forehead with a damp cloth and nodded. "She tried to stay awake because she was worried about you, but she fell asleep on the couch...I carried her to her bedroom and tucked her in."

"Good."

James lifted the pad over Tim's upper wound. "Top one's pretty well stopped bleeding." He checked the bottom one and grimaced. "The other is still bubbling some."

Timothy tried to breathe, but only managed a shallow breath. "Doesn't matter much." He closed his eyes tight for a moment, and then looked up at Jim. "Know...know I'm not going to make it, brother."

"You don't know that...Stop talking foolishness...Now, hang in there...hear me?"

Timothy slowly shook his head back and forth. "Time's running out, brother. We...we both seen men in the Boer War with...with lung shots...It's a downhill...slide."

"Can I do anything?"

He looked up at James again and nodded. "I...I think I died for a bit...out there before...before you came out..."

James frowned. "Do what? Died? What do you mean?"

Tim groaned a little. "Just that...Know I died...because...because I saw Jesus...I saw him."

James leaned closer to hear his brother better. "I don't understand."

Tim grabbed James's arm as his eyes filled with tears. "I saw him...just as clear as I see you...He talked to me."

"What did he say?" He put his other hand on top of Tim's that was fiercely gripping his arm.

His brother closed his eyes for a long moment. "He...wanted me to make amends."

"Amends?"

Tim nodded. "For all that...that money we stole...and the lives we cost."

"They weren't supposed to do that."

"Doesn't matter...they did it...and we're the blame."

James thought for a moment. "What do you want me to do?"

"We...we got ten thousand, five hundred on the last job...Was a lot more, but...but, they couldn't carry all the gold."

James nodded. "All the rest of the money is under the boards, at the bottom of the cooler in the kitchen…And?…What am I supposed to do? I just don't understand."

"Gotta give it back…every dime…Give it back…We can't give those lives back…But, we can what was stolen…We were wrong."

James nodded. "All right…I will…You know I will."

"And you have…have to help see that those…those shiners are eliminated, Brother…all of them." He closed his eyes and pursed his lips against the pain. "They are…are the personification of…of evil…The devil's pawns. He said…said they are…a true scourge…and must…must be cleansed…You will have…He will help."

Tim tried to breathe again and moaned deeply.

"Brother!"

"You have to do…do it…I promised Him." He squeezed James arm again.

"All right, Brother. I'll do it…You know you can count on me…But, what about Elizabeth if I turn myself in?"

"He will provide…He said Maggie…"

Timothy gasped, and then softly sighed his death rattle, "Ahhh."

His hand on James' arm relaxed.

"Brother…Brother…" James leaned over and held him for a long time.

HORSE ISLAND

The fog still lay heavy over the water, but the early morning rising sun was creating a bright glow.

Loraine had stoked up the fire and put two coffee pots on to boil when Silke rolled out of her soogan and laced up her tall Apache style moccasins.

She stood to her feet and ambled over to the fire. "Coffee smells good…Nothin' like it in the mornin'."

Bear Dog got up from his spot beside Silke's bedroll, stretched, and followed her over to the campfire.

Bone and Padrino were next to saunter over after taking care of their morning business out in the woods.

"Morning, babe." He kissed Loraine on the cheek and turned his head. "Got butt breath."

"I know…Now that you're finally up, I need more firewood…No coffee till you bring some…you too, Padrino."

Bone turned toward the woods. "Slave driver."

Padrino was right on his heels. "No, Bone…Blackmailer."

"Right…Both."

Farmer limped over with his cane as Bone and Padrino left camp. "Mornin' all." He looked around at the tents. "Kids still asleep, I see."

Clay stuck his head out from between the flaps of his tent on his hands and knees. Sleep was evident on his face.

"I'm up, I'm up…a little." He blinked, came on out of the tent, got to his feet and rubbed his face with both hands. "Wow, slept hard."

"Need coffee?" Loraine asked.

Clay blinked again. "Thought you'd never ask…That's what woke me up…smellin' the coffee."

He stumbled over to the fire and took the cup Loraine proffered to him, blew across the top and took a sip. "Mmm, nectar of the gods."

Daisy shoved her way out of the tent and made it over to the fire next to Clay. She held her hands out like a beggar. "Coffee? Coffee for the needy?…Coffee?"

Silke chuckled and handed her a steaming cup. "Sustenance an' stimulant for m'lady." She made a half bow.

"It's gracious ye are, sweet lady." Daisy took the cup and held it in both hands, absorbing the warmth.

A hollow-eyed, drawn faced, Etta, was next to come out of her tent.

"How are you feelin' this mornin', Etta?" asked Silke. "Would you like some coffee?"

She nodded. "I'm better…Thanks to you." Etta attempted a smile.

Angel, Eli, and Jen staggered out of their tent and made their way to the fire with the others.

Bone and Padrino walked out of the fog with armloads of deadfall and blowdown and dropped it near the fire.

Bone glanced around. "Where's Maggie?"

"She went hunting and was going to check on what the shiners were doing," commented Loraine. "Said she didn't trust them."

Bone looked at his wife from above his cup. "You think?" He glanced at the others. "Believe we ought to go see about that firefight last night...Got a hunch it may have something to do with the good Mister McPherson."

Loraine nodded. "Don't believe in coincidence."

Silke wrapped her kerchief around the handle of one of the coffee pots and refilled her cup. "Have to agree with you there, Loraine."

"McPherson?" Marshal Farmer had a puzzled look on his face for a moment. "Oh, right...With all the excitement I forgot that was the other reason ya'll are here besides lookin' for the kids."

"Sure glad ya'll came, dad." Clay took a sip of his coffee. "Ya'll too." He glanced at Bone, Silke, Loraine, and Padrino.

Loraine stirred the big skillet of bacon sizzling over the fire, blanketing the immediate area with it's tantalizing fragrance. "We were already on the way when we got the telegram from Marshal Farmer."

She chopped up some potatoes and dumped a couple of cans of beans on top of the bacon and stirred it all together. Bear Dog leaned in to sniff the skillet.

Silke glanced over at her wolf-dog smelling the breakfast and chuckled.

"What's funny, Silke?" asked Bone.

"Oh, it's just somethin' Bass Reeves used to say when we were on the trail when he talked about Marshal Jack McGann's cookin'."

Farmer cocked his head. "And that was?"

"Well, Jack would announce before he started cookin' that everbody had two choices…beans an' bacon or bacon an' beans…What did everbody want?"

Bone grinned. "I always picked bacon an' beans myself."

"That's my favorite, too," added Silke.

Clay and the other teens looked at Silke and Bone in confusion.

"Speakin' of trail, think we should head on down that bayou where Maggie said her dad's cabin was."

Bone nodded. "Agree, Silke." He looked at Padrino and Marshal Farmer. "Why don't ya'll stay here with the kids, in case the shiners come back…Me, Loraine, and Silke can take care of finding McPherson and the little girl plus seeing about Maggie's dad...Think we should go on foot. The horses will make too much noise."

"Agree, Bone," said Padrino. "No need in putting all our eggs in one basket."

Marshal Farmer picked up his tin plate and forked some of Loraine's concoction in it. "Mind we oughta send Clay an' Eli back into town to Murphy's on a couple of the horses, then, an' bring their mounts an' the mule back out while we're waitin'...Agree that Padrino an' me can take care of the shiner's, should they come back."

Marshal Farmer glanced over at Clay and Eli. "You boys stay alert, hear? It is Friday the thirteenth, you know."

Bone chuckled again.

"What's funny about Friday the thirteenth, Bone?...Just a superstition." asked Silke.

"Oh, just something else Jack McGann used to say."

Padrino frowned. "What was that?"

Bone grinned. "Said he didn't believe in superstition...thought it was bad luck."

§§§

CHAPTER SIXTEEN

LUCIUS WELLMAN'S CLINIC

Doctor Wellman's nurse, Hilda, tucked in the bottom corner of the clean sheet she had just put on Ranger Riley Boston's bed. The somewhat heavyset, fiftyish, long time nurse to Doctor

Wellman was replacing his bedding after giving him his morning sponge bath.

Her head snapped to the right to look at his face—the wounded ranger's lips were moving. She leaned over closer and put her left ear near his face and heard a soft whisper.

"Water...Can I...have some...water?"

His eyes fluttered and opened halfway as he repeated, "Can I have some...water?"

"Yes, you can, dear. You just wait one moment...Be right back."

She turned, quickly strode out of the room and down the hall to Doctor Wellman's office.

"Doctor, he's awake. He asked for water."

"Well, good Lord, woman, get him some."

The sixty year old physician pushed back from his desk, grabbed his stethoscope and headed down the hall to the ranger's room.

Wellman entered the small room, approached the bed and looked down on Riley. He bent over, pushed his lids all the way open, and looked closely into his eyes, and then listened to his heartbeat and respiration with his stethoscope.

Nurse Hilda entered just behind the doctor with a glass tumbler of water and a full ceramic pitcher.

She waited until the doctor finished checking the ranger and for him to step aside.

Hilda bent over, held his head up with her left hand and placed the edge of the glass to his dry lips. "Easy now, honey, not too much."

Riley took several swallows, looked up at her in gratitude and nodded. She removed the glass and set it next to the pitcher on the nightstand beside his bed.

"Better?"

He nodded and winced a little. "Thank you," his answer came out a little hoarse from not using his voice.

Riley blinked several times. "Got a headache...feels like I been kicked in the...head."

Wellman nodded and smiled a little. "You were shot in the head, Ranger...Ball bounced off the side."

"That would do it...I would guess." He looked back at Nurse Hilda.

"Need more water?"

He nodded, but not as hard as before.

"Glad you didn't lose your sense of humor, Ranger."

Hilda held the glass to his lips again. This time, he drained it and sighed.

"I remember now…Is Silke awright?"

The doctor nodded. "She, Bone, and Loraine had to go up to Ardmore for Red Wolf's funeral, and then they went on to Caddo Lake after that McPherson fellow an' Marshal Farmer's son an' his friends who were stranded."

"Dang, what am I missin' out on?…Gotta go help…" He tried to raise up, but fell back and put his hand to his head. "Ahhh!"

"You've been unconscious for five days, Ranger. Got a severe concussion…Was worried about you there for a while…But, you're not goin' anywhere for a week or more…Head traumas are dangerous things…Don't push it."

Riley blinked several times. "Right…Got anything for this headache?" He squinted his eyes.

Wellman turned to his nurse. "Hilda, bring a teaspoon of that new aspirin powder we got from that Bayer company in Germany." He turned back to Boston. "You can take some of that powder…a little bitter, but you can wash it down quickly."

Hilda brought a level teaspoon of a white powder and a fresh glass of water and mixed the powder in, stirring it well.

Riley raised his head a little and opened his mouth. Hilda then held the glass to his lips again and allowed him to drink over half of it. He squinched his face, and then drank the rest.

"Dang, bitter ain't the half of it...Lemme have some more of that water, please."

Hilda filled his glass from the pitcher and held it for him again while he drank. "I'll bring you some good bone broth...I should imagine you're a bit hungry."

"Yessum, you could say that...an' I could use the jakes, you don't mind?"

TAYLOR ISLAND

The fourteen remaining shiner men gathered around Big Daddy at the wide front porch of the ramshackle house they all called home.

The patriarch of the clan was the son of one of the forty-eight survivors of the infamous Donner Party from 1847 who resorted to cannibalism when they were stranded in the Sierra Nevada mountains in winter time—the original party was comprised of eighty-seven individuals.

"Now, you bunch of nabobs, listen to me. I'm the last guy in this part of Texas you want to piss off…an' yer gittin' damn close."

Rooster scratched the dirt with the toe of his worn boot. "But, Big Daddy, we…"

"Shut up, Rooster, you ain't got the brains God give a goose…" He looked back at the others. "Now, here's what yer agonna do…Marvin, you take nine others an' go take care of them teenagers…Want them women…hear? An' Cobb…take the rest an' go git that little girl…Got plans fer her." His eyes blazed as he stared at his brood. "Don't leave nobody alive…Got it?"

HORSE ISLAND

Silke, Bone, and Loraine checked their weapons and ammo supply, glanced at each other and headed across the causeway to the mainland spit with Bear Dog padding alongside.

179

They strode purposely along the game trail that bordered Big Cypress Bayou like Maggie had told them to. She had said that her dad's cabin was on some high ground a little over two miles and was where the bayou emptied into the lake just south of what was called Blind Slough.

CADDO LAKE

Elizabeth wandered into the edge of the woods near the cabin with her rag doll, Sally, under her arm.

"I just know we can find some flowers, Sally...it's spring." She glanced near the edge of the bank bordering the lake. "Oh, look! Daffodils!"

Elizabeth knelt down and started picking the low growing wild yellow flowered daffodils, creating a bouquet of them in her left hand.

"Unka Mack will like them on his grave."

She had cried while she watched her uncle James bury his twin brother Timothy near the garden earlier that morning.

"He liked pretty things, you know…Wish I could put some on mama and papa's graves…She liked daffodils too."

She held the flowers against the little triangle nose stitched from red thread on Sally's round face. "Don't they smell nice?"

Elizabeth walked along the path that followed the bank. "Look, look, look, Sally…Purple flowers!…Think mama called them coneflowers. Don't know why, they're not shaped like a cone."

She picked several and added them to her bouquet. "Now, if we could find some black-eyed Susans…Oh, there's some…"

"Don't need no nigger-toes, kid."

She spun around and looked up at the filthy, odoriferous man wearing an equally filthy brown felt hat.

"Who are you?" She held Sally and the flowers close to her chest.

"Don't matter none…Yer comin' with me." He reached down, grabbed her and jerked her up under his arm.

Elizabeth dropped the flowers and Sally, and screamed before Cobb clamped a dirty hand over her mouth, turned and ran up the path to a pirogue pulled up on the bank.

"Got 'er, ya'll go take care of the man," he ordered Rooster, Wash, and Pie."

Cobb pulled a nasty rag from the pocket of his overalls and stuffed it in Elizabeth's mouth. Then he tied her hands and feet and threw her in the bottom of one of the boats.

He pushed the flat-bottomed jon boat back out into the dark waters of the lake, jumped in, picked up the paddle and started stroking across the lake toward Taylor Island.

Rooster, Wash, and Pie headed along the path in the direction of the McPherson cabin...

§§§

CHAPTER SEVENTEEN

CADDO LAKE

"Elizabeth…Elizabeth, where are you?" James walked behind the barn looking for her.

He had just finished filling in Timothy's grave and realized Elizabeth had wandered off.

"Elizabeth…Answer me. Told you to stay by the house…Elizabeth." He headed to the path that ran along the shore of the lake.

A bullet thudded into the cypress tree beside his head followed immediately by the roar of a big bore rifle.

James ducked, drew his brother's pistol and fired up the trail at the three shiners he could see through the trees. He turned and tried to run back toward the house, but another bullet kicked up dirt and moss growing along the path by his foot. He took cover behind another tree and fired again.

The three shiners all had grins on their faces showing their remaining tobacco-stained teeth as each fired at him with their rifles.

James checked the cylinder of the Russian made handgun. "Five rounds left…gotta get to the house." He peeked around the tree.

One of the big .52 caliber rounds from a shiner's Spencer ricocheted from the side of the hard wood trunk and whined mournfully off into the distance.

James squatted down low and sighted back along the trail. He caught a glimpse of one of the shiners and snapped off another round.

The shot was followed by a yelp of pain.

"Hah, got a piece of one." He turned again and sprinted down the path for ten feet and jumped behind another tree as three rounds peppered it.

"Damn, that was close." He looked around the thick bole to try to get another shot but had to duck back as another bullet glanced off the side of the tree, spraying him with slivers of wood.

He pointed his pistol around the cypress, blindly fired two quick shots, and then ran another ten feet along the trail to the edge of the clearing around the cabin. The large cloud of white gunsmoke he created helped shield him from view until he got to the last tree at the end of the trail.

James looked around for another place of cover closer to the house which was a good twenty yards further—nothing but a large oak next to the structure.

He glanced down at the gun again and shook his head. "Two left...Dang, should have gotten the belt and holster. Would have had fourteen more rounds."

He scouted about his present place of concealment and could see the three men were creeping closer, running from tree to tree like he had. One was limping.

James searched the area again with his eyes. "Where are you, Elizabeth?" Realization suddenly hit him—*Oh, God...they got her.*

"Got to get more ammo..." He pursed his lips and muttered, "Like Farragut said, 'Damn the torpedoes...'"

James fired his last two rounds and sprinted toward the house, zigzagging as he ran. He made it a little over halfway to the cabin when a bullet plowed the packed dirt beside and a little to the front of him. He dove to the ground, rolled to the left.

A fusillade of gunfire roared in the clearing—but it was coming from the side of the cabin in front of him. He belly crawled forward to the big oak, the only tree left in the clearing after he had built the log house and took refuge behind it.

More fire came from the trees in front and to the side, but it wasn't directed at him. He could hear large caliber explosions mixed with rapid fire from a smaller caliber gun from the edge of the cabin.

"What in hell?"

SILKE'S QUEST

A shrill cry of a man in severe pain echoed through the forest—it stopped abruptly in mid-scream.

The exchange of gunfire continued for several moments, and then there was deadly quiet. Clouds of acrid smoke drifted slowly across the clearing, but only from the direction of the trees.

James looked about in total confusion until he saw a woman in buckskins with long strawberry blonde hair in a single thick loose braid drooped over her left shoulder step out from the trees behind him. She was putting a huge handgun in a holster strapped about her shapely hips. A blue-eyed, black wolf trotted alongside her.

He heard a sound from the house and saw a giant of a man along with a comparatively small, very attractive Mexican woman, also both in buckskins, step out from around the corner.

"Need your help, Bone," said Silke.

"What?"

"Can't get my tomahawk out of the head of one of those yahoos…it's stuck…He's in back of that biggest tree back there." She pointed behind her.

Ken Farmer

Bone grinned and shook his head. "Buy you books and buy you books...you still eat the covers."

He walked past James and Silke into the trees. In a short moment he came back out and flipped the warhatchet to Silke.

She caught it by the handle in the air, looked at the blade, smiled and stuck it in her beaded belt. "Thanks...an' thanks for cleanin' the blood off."

"Had brain stuck on it, too...Wiped it on that shiner's overalls...You dang sure buried it deep in the back of his skull all right...Throw it?"

"Uh-huh...From about twenty feet...Bear Dog got him first...Kept him from turnin' 'round an' shootin' me."

"I heard...Well done, missy. You too, Bear Dog."

The wolf-dog sat down next to Silke and raised one paw at Bone.

"You're welcome." The big man looked down at James still lying behind the tree in total confusion. "He had a little bullet hole in his leg, too, Timothy. Most likely from your Nagant...Didn't expect to find you here...We were looking for..."

"I'm not Timothy, I'm James."

Bone lifted his right eyebrow. "Huh?"

"Sounds like a war yonderway." Marshal Farmer looked to the east.

"Bone and them must have come across some of the shiners," said Padrino. "Sounded pretty fierce there for a few minutes…Hard to argue against those .50s. They tend to scare the pee out of the bad guys, especially when they've never seen or heard one…and Loraine's .45 semiautomatic…I'd say she emptied more than one magazine."

"Glad we sent Clay and Eli to town for those mounts." Farmer got to his feet.

"Think they'll be awright, Marshal?"

"Oh, 'spect so, Daisy."

Farmer reached for the coffee pot with one of his folded over gloves. The pot exploded, sending hot coffee spraying up the marshal's arm and the graniteware utensil spinning across the clearing.

"Son of a…" Farmer dove to his right, rolled and came up with his Colt in his hand, pointed back to the other side of the causeway.

He cranked two quick shots at the ball of white gunsmoke that boiled out of the copse of cedar trees.

"Damn fool!" Marvin slapped his younger brother, Coot, with his hat. "Tol' you not to shoot till I said...You cain't hit a bull in the ass with a broom."   He turned to the others. "You bunch of idiots scatter an' start a pickin' 'em off. Don't look like they got mor'n two guns, anyhoo."

The shiners spread out, getting behind the thick cypress trees for cover and started firing into the campsite.

Marshal Farmer crawled over behind a large log they had been sitting on. "Everybody get down!...Angel, where's that other Winchester I gave ya'll?"

"In our tent." She sprinted over to the smaller of the three tents and dove through the flap in front.

In a short moment, she crawled back out with the rifle in one hand and a box of shells in the other—she wormed her way over to the same twelve-foot log Marshal Farmer was behind.

"Know how to use that thing, Little Bit?"

"Yessir. My daddy taught me."

"Then get to it...Shoot at the center of the fresh clouds of gunsmoke. Might get lucky...an' keep your head down between shots."

Angel levered a round in the chamber, laid the Winchester on top of the log and squeezed off a round at the newest gunsmoke cloud across the causeway.

Her shot was followed by a yell of pain.

"Hit somebody, girl...Good job." Farmer snapped off two more shots at another cloud...it too was followed by a scream.

Padrino worked his way closer to the waterway and took cover behind a cypress and laid down to present a smaller target. He scanned the other side and picked one of the shiners he could see part of.

He triple tapped his Colt 1911A semiautomatic .45. It sounded like one shot.

The man on the other side yelled out, spun around, fell to the side of his tree, kicked out for the next twenty seconds with his left foot drumming a tattoo on the forest floor—then fell still.

Padrino grinned. "That's one."

"What in hell kinda gun did that old man have what shot Lute?…Couldn't even count the shots it wuz so fast," asked Doodle. "An' where'd that split-tail come up with a repeater?"

"How the duce should I know?" Marvin ducked back behind his tree as two of Farmer's .45 rounds thunked into the wood in rapid succession.

Bone's head snapped back to the west. "Damn, they hit the camp too…Let's go."

"Have to find my niece, sorry I can't go to help." James got to his feet.

"Elizabeth?" asked Silke.

James nodded. "Think the shiners took her."

"We'll meet you at their island. That's where they would have taken her." Bone cocked his head listening to the gunfire in the distance. "Gotta go check on the rest of our people."

"Understand...Have a pirogue. I'll come at them from the lake."

"Don't let 'em see you...They're a nasty bunch."

James looked at Silke and set his jaw. "I know."

"Have a rifle?" asked Loraine.

He nodded. "And a double barreled twelve gauge."

"Take both...and plenty ammo," added Silke.

"No such thing," muttered Bone.

She glanced at the big man. "Oh, right."

"Let's move out, people." Bone turned and headed back west along the game trail that ran alongside Big Cypress Bayou at a jog.

Silke, Bear Dog, and Loraine were right behind him.

They could hear the continued firefight from Horse Island nearly two miles ahead of them. Bone lengthened his lead over the girls while Bear Dog easily kept pace with the long-legged inactive Marine along the narrow path.

The gunfire abruptly stopped...

§§§

CHAPTER EIGHTEEN

TAYLOR ISLAND

Cobb pulled the pirogue up on the bank, removed the dirty rag from Elizabeth's mouth and cut the ropes from her hands and feet. He grabbed her arm and jerked her out of the boat.

"Ow," she screamed. "You're hurtin' me."

"You don't know hurt, kid…Shut up."

He pulled and dragged her stumbling and falling over to the main house and up the steps to the porch where Big Daddy was sitting in his rocking chair.

"Here you go, Big Daddy...fresh meat."

"Come here, girl." He leaned forward in his chair.

Tobacco juice stained both corners of his mouth and down into his rough, dark brown beard, tinged with gray on each side of his chin.

Cobb pushed her forward close enough for the patriarch to grab her arm and pull her up to him.

She turned her head at the stench of his fetid breath.

Big Daddy roared with laughter. "What's the matter, girl, don't like 'baccer?"

"It stinks."

"You'll get used to it."

Elizabeth shook her head. "I don't think so."

He laughed again. "How old 're you?"

She stood up straight with her chin in the air. "I'm nine and a half years old."

The grizzled leader of the clan nodded. "Old enough."

"For what?"

"You'll see." A malevolent grin spread across his face. "Yes, indeedee, you'll see."

He spat a stream of the noxious tobacco juice to the side of the porch and looked at Cobb. "Where's yer brothers?"

"They stayed to take care of that guy."

"No," Elizabeth shouted. "You better not."

"Oh, an' why's that, little miss smart mouth?" asked Cobb.

"He's my Unka James an' he'll kill them. He was in the war."

"What war?" asked Big Daddy.

"Well, uh…I don't know, but he was a fighter in a war."

Big Daddy glanced at Cobb again with a fierce glare. "Heard a bunch of shootin' from thataway 'fore you got here an' it wadn't jest Rooster, Wash, an' Pie's Spencers neither." He paused in thought for a minute. "Best git back in the boat an' go see to 'em."

Everyone in camp turned and looked to the north at the sounds of gunfire.

Big Daddy grinned, spat another amber stream of tobacco juice off the porch, not bothering with the dribble, and nodded. "Now that sounds more like it...Marvin's bunch."

They could hear the sounds of semiautomatic .45 fire plus a Winchester rifle as it was added to the mix.

HORSE ISLAND

Bone and Bear Dog ran up to the causeway, followed a couple of minutes later by Silke and Loraine—each had their sidearms in their hands.

They carefully looked around the area on the mainland side.

"See two bodies over here to the left."

"Got one more on this side, Bone," replied Silke.

They stepped closer and checked the bodies.

Bone bent over each one. "Both dead, here."

Silke did the same while Loraine stood guard, watching behind them.

"Same here...This one has three bullet wounds."

Loraine glanced at the body along with Bear Dog sniffing the blood. "From Padrino's .45."

Bone cupped his hands around his mouth. "Hello the camp."

"That you, Bone?"

"No, it's Robin Hood and his merry ladies, Padrino."

"Figured…Come ahead."

The three and Bear Dog waded across the waterway to the island as Padrino, Daisy, Angel, and Jen came forward to meet them.

Marshall Farmer remained seated on his log near the fire.

"Looks like ya'll acquitted yourselves well," said Loraine. "Anybody hurt?"

"I'd say…We're all good," replied Padrino as they walked over to where Farmer was sitting.

"Welcome back," the marshal said. "Didn't see any sense of gettin' up an' hobblin' over to meet ya'll. Figured Padrino and the kids could do that fine."

"Don't blame you," replied Silke.

"Looks like the shiners are down six. We took care of three over to Maggie's dad's cabin," said Loraine.

"See Timothy and Elizabeth, Bone?" asked Padrino.

"Apparently the shiners killed Timothy, but met Maggie's father, James…Tim's twin brother."

"Say what?" asked Farmer. "Timothy has a twin?"

Silke nodded. "Shiners hit the cabin last night and killed Tim…he got one of them." She looked around the camp. "Maggie not back?"

Padrino picked up the coffee pot the shiners shot and looked at the finger-sized hole in the side and shook his head. "Haven't seen her since she went over to check on the shiner's island."

Bone and Silke exchanged glances.

"We better head that way." Silke looked at Bone and then the others. "Shiners got Elizabeth."

"Who's Elizabeth?" asked Daisy.

"Timothy and James' niece…she's nine years old," replied Silke.

"No," screamed Etta, who had been sitting quietly on the log next to Marshal Farmer. "No!…You have to get her…You can't let those animals have her!" She got to her feet, with the blanket held about her—shaking like a leaf.

Silke stepped over and put her arm around the teen's shoulder. "We know, honey. We'll get her…" She glanced back at Bone and Loraine.

"...an' take care of those inbreds while we're at it...Don't worry."

Bone opened his saddlebags, took out the rest of his ammo for his S & W 500 and dropped it into his parfleche. "You okay, Pard?" He looked at Loraine.

"Ya'll give me a minute to reload these two empty mags to bring me back up to four plus what's in my Kimber, an' I'm good to go."

He turned to Silke. "How much you got?"

"Just what's in my belt an' this box of rounds Buck Stienke made for me." She opened her saddlebags, took it out and held it up, and then put it in her pouch.

Bone nodded. "We can share if you run low."

She grinned. "Got my war hatchet, too."

The big man smiled and nodded again. "May have to get me one of those...Pretty damn good for close combat."

"You think?" commented Loraine.

"I'll stay here with the girls...just slow you up," said Marshal Farmer.

"How's your ammo?" asked Bone.

"I'm good...Got an extra box for the Winchester, too...Angel's a crack shot."

Bone held up his thumb to the attractive golden-eyed blonde and winked. She blushed and grinned back at him.

"Clay and Eli should be back in a couple hours," Farmer added. "Clay's got his Peacemaker an' Eli has the other Winchester."

Bone picked up a canteen and took a long drink. "Let's go...Take us a little over an hour to get to the shiner's island."

Angel handed Bone a big handful of peppered jerky. "Put this in your pouch...need to eat somethin' 'fore ya'll get there."

"Thanks, Little Bit. Always good to eat when you get the chance...never know when the next opportunity will come by." He bent over and gave her a hug.

CADDO LAKE

James walked along the path that ran beside the lake looking for signs of Elizabeth. He stopped abruptly and knelt down in the grass to the right of the trail and picked up a small rag doll.

"Sally." He looked in the grass next to where the doll had been. "Wild flowers…she was picking wild flowers for Timothy's grave," he muttered as he picked up the bunch of daffodils along with some purple cone flowers and nodded.

James saw a man's flat-heeled boot prints in the soft earth of the trail while Elizabeth's small prints disappeared—he picked her up, they headed south.

"Going to his boat."

James spun on his heel and trotted back to the cabin, stopping briefly to lay her flowers on his brother's grave. "Elizabeth wanted you to have these, Brother."

He quickly crossed himself, kissed the silver cross necklace around his neck, and then headed inside to get his weapons and ammunition.

Ten minutes later, James dipped his paddle in the water on the right side of the wooden pirogue in a J-stroke to keep the flat-bottomed craft headed in a straight line.

The morning fog had fairly well thinned over land, wisps of it remained across the dark water. James was trying to keep inside the line of the mists and come to shore on the mainline over a hundred yards north of the shiner's island.

He could see the tendrils of smoke rising from their camp fires as well as their main still. Then he squinted his eyes and could make out another pirogue gliding across the water back in the direction of his cabin—a shiner. He sculled his craft sideways to the right to get deeper into the fog, and then continued.

The swamp boat moved silently across the placid, glasslike surface of the exotic primordial lake until he neared the shore. James stroked hard two more times to run the bow up on the land.

He got up, slung his rifle's sling over his left shoulder, his ammo bag over his right, and carried his shotgun in his left hand as he stepped out of the boat to the shore. James leaned down, grabbed the gunwale and dragged the lightweight craft further up on the bank.

A pair of green eyes watched him from the brush as he secured the boat, and then they disappeared back into the foliage…

§§§

CHAPTER NINETEEN

CADDO LAKE

Eli looked over at the bayou on the right and the eerie lake on the left. "Think we're about there?"

Clay pointed off to the northeast across a bay of the lake. "That's Horse Island 'cross the way there where camp is…'Bout another forty-five minutes or so, I reckon."

The two teens were trailing the same six horses for the girls and themselves they had ridden out to the island, plus the pack mule. Clay held the lead rope to a string of three horses and the mule, while Eli led the other three horses.

Eli looked in his possibles pouch for a piece of jerky. "I could eat the sideboards out of a gut wagon…all my jerky's gone."

"As I recall, you ate it all on the way into town…an' you had breakfast before we left."

"I'm a growin' boy."

"Uh-huh."

"You got any left?"

"Do."

"Wanna share?"

"No."

"That's not nice."

"Didn't take you to raise."

Forty minutes later, they crossed the causeway to the island. It was down to only five or six inches deep.

Clay and Eli dismounted and led the animals over to the graze area and pulled the tack on the two horses belonging to Loraine and Padrino they had ridden to town and back. They still had all the saddles they had removed when they set up camp.

Marshal Farmer limped over to where they were on his cane. "Any problems, boys?"

"None at all, Pop…'cept Eli ate all his jerky an' then wanted some of mine…" Clay glanced around the camp. "Where's the others an' Bear Dog?"

"Well, that's the thing, bub…we got attacked by those shiners while ya'll were gone…killed three of 'em…They went over to their island to finish 'em off an' rescue a nine year old little girl."

"No, lie?" exclaimed Eli.

Farmer looked over at the teen with a raised brow. "What I said, idn't it?"

Eli looked down at the ground. "Yessir."

Clay pulled his Peacemaker and checked the rounds. "They're gonna need another gun." He turned and headed toward the waterway.

Daisy caught up with him, put her arms around his neck, gave him a hug, and then kissed him. "You be careful, hard head."

Clay kissed her back and nodded.

"Now, hold on, boy. You don't need to be goin'...Those inbreds are killers."

Clay turned to his father. "Dad, I'm near grown...Old as you were when you were fightin' the Injuns...Not gonna talk about it...goin' to go help Bone an' them."

The marshal stared at him—he had no answer.

Clay waded across the water.

Marshal Farmer yelled after him. "Watch your back, son."

"Plan to, dad." He disappeared into the dark, foreboding woods and hanging Spanish moss on the mainland.

Bear Dog padded along the game trail and abruptly stopped. A low growl rumbled from the bottom of his throat, and the hair along his back raised.

Silke stepped up beside him and put her hand on his neck. "What is it, boy?"

His gaze was directed on a clump of juniper ahead and to the left of the trail. He took one stiff-legged step forward, and then another.

"Appreciate it if you hold that creature, Miss," came a voice from the copse.

"Easy, Bear Dog." She put her hand on his shoulders.

James stepped out on the trail, he carried his double barrel shotgun in his left hand and his Henry was slung across his back by a leather thong. "Thought he might remember me."

"He does. Just didn't like you hidin' in the trees." Silke smiled.

Bone walked forward. "Just get here?"

"Few minutes ago...Saw one of the shiners paddling back toward my place...Stayed inside the fog bank so he couldn't see me."

Bone nodded. "Probably going to check on the others...He'll be back." He indicated Padrino. "This is my godfather, Padrino...Don't let his age fool you."

"What age, Bone?...Watch your mouth." The retired Marine glared at him.

James grinned. "His eyes already told me that...Got a plan?"

"Sort of," interjected Silke. She looked at Bone. "What say James an' I cross the waterway with Bear Dog, enter the north end of their island?...An' ya'll cross an' go in on the south..."

Loraine interrupted her. "We meet in the middle."

Silke glanced at James. "We'll go for Elizabeth…"

"And we'll create a diversion and pull them to the south," added Padrino. "Classic military move."

James nodded. "There's a tin shed up near their house…"

"Seen it," said Bone. "What's it for?"

"It's got a bunch of dynamite and their inventory of moonshine stored in it. The shiners use the dynamite to kill gators and fish by throwing it in the water…"

"Yeah." Bone had an enigmatic smile on his face. "Do that in our ti…uh, where we're from too. Stuns them…Illegal as hell…You going to do what I think you're going to do?"

James pursed his lips. "After we get my niece…if we can."

"No if to it, Mister McPherson…No if to it," said Silke. "I made a promise to take care of her a while back…Not accustomed to breakin' my word."

James looked first at Bone, and then at Silke. "Just so ya'll know. My brother and I orchestrated those railroad robberies through our sister's husband. He didn't know anything about it...Know that's why ya'll came."

"You were involved, too?" asked Silke.

He nodded. "We were going to go out to California with the money." He took a breath. "When Timothy was dyin', he said he saw Jesus...Talked to him...Made me promise to give it all back...Nobody was supposed to die...Swear to God, nobody was supposed to die..."

"But, they did," interrupted Bone.

A sincere look of consternation and guilt crossed James' face. "I know, an' we can't bring them back...but we can at least return all the money." He looked off into the dark woods. "Case I don't come back...I left a note under a can of Arbuckles on the cabinet in the kitchen back at the house...Says where all the money and gold is hidden."

"We'll take care of it," commented Loraine.

Silke glanced about. "Wonder where Ma..."

Bear Dog spun around to face back down the trail, growling once again.

Bone, Loraine, Padrino, and Silke drew their weapons and held them at the ready as the six foot, eighteen year old Marshal Farmer's son jogged into view around a bend in the path.

"Clay, what are you doing here?" asked Bone.

"You need another gun."

"This is going to be dangerous work," said Silke.

He nodded. "I know."

"You any good with that?" Padrino indicated the Colt strapped around his hips.

"Yessir."

"Well, I hope so," added Bone. "You'll come with us, then. We're headed to the south end of the island...Silke and James are going to the north." He looked at them, then back at Clay. "Their job is to get the little girl...ours is to take care of as many shiners as we can...Near as we can guess, there's ten to twelve left."

Clay's jaw muscles rippled, and his blue eyes snapped. "They killed my best friend, Deputy Bone...I..."

"Don't have to say anymore, son," Silke glanced around at the others. "Know what you mean."

"All right, people, let's do this." Bone looked at Silke and James. "Ya'll get into position, but don't do anything till you hear gunfire from our end…Then do what you have to do."

Silke smiled. "Consider it done."

"Good luck."

"Lucks got nothin' to do with it, Loraine," Silke checked the loads in her .50 cal pistol. "God help those bastards."

The two parties separated. Silke, James, and Bear Dog entered the brush and headed in the direction of the edge of the lake. Bone, Loraine, Padrino, and Clay disappeared down the trail to the south.

Bear Dog struck out paddling in the black water across the twenty yards to the island—Silke and James quietly waded through the waist-deep water behind him.

They crept up the bank in a grove of willows. Bear Dog shook to rid his black coat of excess water.

"Let's ease up to the clearing around their camp an' wait for Bone's signal." Silke looked off to the west. "Goin' to be sundown in about thirty minutes."

James nodded. "That's a good thing…be a lot more shadows."

They worked their way through the scattered big cypress trees and underbrush until they were at the edge of the clearing with the tin storage shed between them and the long shotgun style homeplace of the shiner's.

Silke and James hunkered down behind a low growing, blooming, Osage orange—commonly called a horse-apple tree. Bear Dog laid down beside Silke—all his senses alert.

The relative still air of the swamp was suddenly rent with the shrill, piercing scream of a child…

§§§

CHAPTER TWENTY

CADDO LAKE

Bone, Loraine, Padrino, and Clay made their way
along the game trail toward the south end of Taylor
Island.

The late afternoon shadows were lengthening,
making the swamp even more spooky.

"Still don't understand where Maggie is."

Bone glanced back at Loraine. "Bet she's about somewhere...Girl hates those shiners."

"I know. Wish we had the whole story."

"Think there's a story?"

Loraine nodded. "Gut hunch is all, Padrino...Gut hunch."

Bone grinned. "Always go with your gut..."

He stopped abruptly in the middle of the trail as Maggie stepped out from behind a tree. Loraine almost bumped into his back, while Clay ran into Padrino.

"Dang, girl, you're like an Indian or a ghost...I'm pretty hard to sneak up on."

Her green eyes sparkled as a grin spread across her alabaster face which made the scattering of freckles across her nose scrunch up.

"Sorry, Bone, didn't mean to frighten ya'll. The swamp is my special place...I can walk right up to a deer or a raccoon or just about any creature."

"Find out anything?" asked Loraine.

Maggie nodded. "They're pretty upset 'bout some of 'em gettin' kilt. The leader, old man Zeke Carter...heard most of the boys call him Big Daddy...he's fit to be tied."

Padrino grinned. "Things not going his way?"

"Think you could say that…He's takin' it out on the rest…'cludin' the women folk."

"Are the women all his offspring, too?" asked Loraine.

Maggie shook her head. "Only a couple, plus his first wife…most have been stolen an' are locked up at night so's they can't run off."

Bone frowned. "Why hasn't the law been out and done something about it?"

She looked a the big man. "They're a scared to…Several have tried…Never seen again."

"That's fixing to come to a screechin' halt," said Bone.

Maggie scuffed the moss on the trail at their feet with the toe of her moccasin. "Big Daddy has my cousin."

"Your cousin?" asked Loraine.

"Uh-huh…Elizabeth is my cousin."

"Oh, right. Hadn't put all that together."

"She's so small, surely they don't intend to…"

Maggie interrupted Loraine, "She's big enough to breed."

"What?" Loraine put her hand to her mouth. "You don't mean he's…"

"Yes, ma'am, he's goin' to make her one of his wives."

Padrino leaned his head against the trunk of a tree. "My God in Heaven…That despicable…"

"All the women folk are his wives…Even his young grand daughters."

Clay bent over. "Think I'm gonna be sick."

"The practice of pedophilia and taking child brides is acceptable for one of the world's major religions," offered Padrino.

"It's not a religion," hissed Bone. "It's a self-aggrandizing cult…under the false guise of religion."

"The shiners don't believe in anyone or thing but themselves," said Maggie.

"Add atheism to pedophilia, incest, and cannibalism, an' you have the shiners," commented Clay. "The murderin' bastards have to be eliminated."

Bone glanced at Clay, then at Maggie and nodded. "Your dad said Jesus told your uncle when he was dyin'…the shiners were the personification of evil…The devil's pawns. He said they were a scourge, and had to be cleansed…"

Bone was interrupted by Elizabeth's bloodcurdling scream from the island. "Oh, damn…" He looked at his godfather. "Well, Master Gunns, like Gunny Highway in *Heartbreak Ridge* said, 'Improvise, adapt, and overcome'…Let's go."

They moved through the brush to the edge of the waterway between the island and the mainland.

Bone stepped out into the dark waters. "Spread out and try to be quiet. We're sittin' ducks till we get to the other side."

They waded quickly as they could through the chilly water until they clambered up on the bank.

"Padrino, you and Loraine take the flank like we did with the Rudabaugh gang in Jacksboro…Clay and I will take point. Crossfire with your .45 semiautomatics will be devastating. We'll pick up the stragglers…Questions?" He glanced at Clay.

The young man shook his head.

"Check your loads."

Clay slipped his Colt from the holster, pulled the hammer to half-cock and spun the cylinder.

Bone looked at him again. "Five or six?"

"Five."

"Add another."

218

Clay nodded, eased a round from his belt and slipped it into the empty chamber in the cylinder and snapped the gate closed. "Ready."

Bone looked around again for Maggie. "Now, where did…"

Elizabeth screamed again.

"Move, people."

The four spread out to their positions and moved forward at a quickstep.

Silke grimaced at Elizabeth's second scream. "Go, Bear Dog…Find her."

The black beast disappeared in the blink of an eye into the shadows, at Silke's urging, but in a straight line for the long shotgun house.

She and James separated right and left, and then moved forward.

The sound of heavy gunfire echoed from the south end of the island—some rapid fire, single .45 shots, and the heavy boom of a .50 caliber could easily be heard.

The shiners were standing around the three campfires, drinking some of their own wares from light colored earthenware jugs, grabbed their long guns leaned against trees and sprinted south toward the sounds.

Only three women were tending pots at the fires while the rest, along with the children, were in their wooden cages located over in the woods a little distance from the house.

Silke, with her .50 cal in her right hand and her tomahawk in her left, sprinted directly for the house as she saw a black blur jump from the ground to the porch and into the open doorway.

James carried his double-barreled shotgun in both hands—his Henry was still slung across his back. He was headed toward the tin storage building.

A woman-like scream reverberated from inside the long house—but it was, in reality, a man.

Ab and Anse Carter happened to see James running toward the camp from the woods.

"Looky yonder, Ab." Anse turned, raised his Springfield to his shoulder and fired.

James staggered two steps, then another, and then fell to his face in the dirt, three feet from the shed.

It took a second for the gunsmoke to clear enough for Anse to see his results. "Got 'em...Let's go see what all that fuss is at the other end of the island."

"Ahead of you, Anse," said Ab.

The two shiners ran to catch up to their brothers in the deepening shadows of the gloaming.

Silke, seeing James fall, snapped a shot at Anse with her S&W 500.

The shiner's head exploded like a ripe watermelon in a massive cloud of pink tinged with red, gray, and white chunks as his body flipped over backward from the impact of the 500 grain slug.

Ab stumbled and fell to the ground as he was being covered in bloody gore. He looked at Silke as he scrambled to get to his feet, but another pink mist blew out of his back as she drilled him in the middle of his chest. He rolled over twice, both legs kicked out for several seconds before death quickly recruited him also.

After firing the shots to get attention of the camp, Bone, Loraine, Padrino, and Clay quickly reloaded.

Doodle and Pickle led the group of nine shiners coming across the partial clearing from the camp proper. They each carried a Spencer or Springfield rifle. Behind them came Willy, Fats, Ancil, and three others, also similarly armed.

Padrino and Loraine spread out to the flanks. Both knelt down and poured a withering crossfire toward the oncoming shiners from their .45 semiautomatics—rapidly emptying a full clip each.

"Lie down, boy," Bone yelled at Clay.

The young man did as he was told and cranked off several shots from the prone position.

The dirt around him exploded as a couple of the big caliber rounds from the Spencers plowed craters from near misses.

Clay cried out and rolled to his left.

Bone spun around at the sound. "You hit?"

"No, sir! Got dirt in my eyes." He brought both hands up in an attempt to clear them.

Bone squeezed the trigger at Doodle, scoring a center mass shot that blew a chunk of red out of his back, spraying his brother Fats behind him.

Doodle stumbled backward into Fats, taking him down too.

A bullet from one of the shiners tugged at Bone's parfleche pouch while another took his green John Bull hat from his head.

"Damn, that pisses me off."

He raised both massive arms in the air and let out with the same yell he had used to imitate the *Sasquatch* before—it echoed across the lake.

The rest of the horde threw on their brakes, sliding to stops.

"It's them!…Run!" one of them yelled.

"Oh, God…Oh, God," others were screaming.

They had no qualms leaving their brother's bodies scattered about. Fats had crawled out from under Doodle and ran to catch up with his brothers.

There was an answering cry across the lake.

Silke cleared the four steps up to the porch in one bound and barreled through the doorway. She spied the patriarch of the clan standing at the edge of a cornhusk bed where Elizabeth lay crumpled and still.

Bear Dog had Big Daddy's arm in his jaws—the man's grizzled face was gashed and torn in several places as was his shoulder. The leader of the shiners was trying to sling the young half-wolf off. Blood was spraying everywhere.

"Kill him, Bear Dog!"

"Damn you, woman." Carter pulled a Navy Colt from the holster at his hips with his off hand, and held it against Bear Dog's head.

"No, you bastard!"

Silke slung the war hatchet sideways at the hulk of a man. The razor sharp weapon caught him at the junction of his nose and forehead. The force and momentum of the tomahawk sheared the top half of his skull off—both the warhawk and the piece of skull landed behind him on the bed next to Elizabeth's form.

Big Daddy, already dead, tottered for a moment, and then collapsed straight down like a pile of dirty laundry to the planks of the filthy floor.

Silke ran over, picked up Elizabeth's limp body and held her to her chest…

§§§

CHAPTER TWENTY-ONE

TAYLOR ISLAND

James slowly got to his feet using the side of the corrugated tin shed to steady himself. His shirt was soaked with blood, and he still had his shotgun in his left hand.

He looked around, trying to comprehend what happened, and saw Silke step out of the shiner's shotgun shack with Elizabeth in her arms.

"Run, Silke...Run," he shouted as loudly as he could.

Her head snapped up and she spied James leaning against the side of the storage shed.

He staggered forward two steps and grabbed the latch to the door. "Run...run!"

Silke instantly realized what he was doing, jumped from the porch to the ground and headed to the woods between the camp and the shore, west of the clearing—running as fast as she could, carrying the unconscious Elizabeth.

She came up on the cage holding the captive women and the children. Silke pulled her tomahawk and slashed the rope tying the door closed.

"Get away...Run to the mainland!...Hurry."

The raggedy, malnourished women grabbed their equally raggedy children and followed Silke's instructions.

She sprinted on to the shore, waded into the waist deep water, and crossed the waterway.

Bone, Loraine, Padrino, and Clay followed the five remaining shiners to the camp.

At the edge of the clearing, Bone was able to see James grab the latch to the door to the shed, pull it open and fall inside.

"Waterway!...Go...Go." He turned and led the group through the woods to the shore of the island on the mainland side.

They splashed into the water, wading as fast as they could across the twenty yards separating the island from the mainland.

James collapsed to the dirt floor of the shed. The entire back side of the building was stacked floor to ceiling with wooden cases marked 'DYNAMITE' on one side and shelves of earthenware jugs of high content alcohol moonshine.

He rolled over to his back and looked up at the tin ceiling—delirium was taking over. "My brother's calling me, I can hear him...I'm coming Brother...I'm coming."

James pointed the twelve gauge shotgun at the dynamite less than a foot away, and pulled both triggers…

The fiery impact of the double ought shot detonated the explosives—the moonshine added to the conflation…

The very ground of the island shook with the massive explosion that flattened everything within a hundred yards of the building—including the house and nearby trees. The surviving male shiners were incinerated.

Across the waterway, Silke had joined up with Bone's group. They turned toward the island at the deafening explosion and could see the massive fireball boiling up into the atmosphere high over the tree tops.

Silke watched the small mushroom cloud of fire, smoke, and debris grow above the trees. "God works in mysterious ways…His wonders to perform."

Bone nodded. "James said Jesus told his brother that He would help."

Elizabeth stirred in Silke's arms. "What happened?" She looked up at her. The side of her little face was red. "The bad man hit me."

Silke held her closely. "I know, honey...He'll never hurt you again...He'll never hurt anyone again."

"Unka James?"

Silke looked over at Bone and Loraine. "He went to be with your Uncle Mack, honey."

"An' momma and daddy, too?"

"Yes, baby...your momma and daddy, too."

Elizabeth's eyes filled with tears. "What's goin' to happen to me?...I...I don't...have anybody..."

She choked and buried her face in Silke's bosom. Her frail little body shook with her sobs.

Tears ran down Silke's face, too. "Yes, you do, baby, yes, you do...You'll have me."

"And me," said Loraine.

"Me, too," added Bone.

"All of us, Elizabeth," commented Padrino.

Elizabeth sniffed and turned her tear filled eyes up to Silke and then the others. "Ya'll...ya'll love...me?"

"Yes, baby, I love you." Silke looked at the others. "We all do."

Loraine tried to wipe the tears from her eyes as she looked over at Bone—who was doing the same thing.

Padrino pursed his lips together and brushed the tears from his face. Clay turned away to hide his.

Elizabeth sniffed and took a ragged breath. "I need my Sally."

Silke glanced at Bone.

The big man touched the side of Elizabeth's face tenderly. "We have to go to your Uncle James' house, bet we find it there."

She almost smiled and nodded.

"Let's head back to camp first, then over to the cabin," said Silke. "Need to check out that information James gave us."

"Works for me." Bone turned and led the way back to their camp.

HORSE ISLAND

Bone picked Elizabeth up and carried her across the shallow causeway into camp with Bear Dog splashing at his side. Loraine, Silke, Padrino, and

Clay followed behind. He set her down when they reached the other side.

"Glad to see ya'll back." Marshal Farmer got to his feet to hug Clay. "Awright, son?"

"Yessir, just got dirt in my eyes from a near miss, is all."

He nodded. "Near miss...Good as a mile."

"We have to go check on that cabin again," said Silke. "Elizabeth needs her Sally doll."

"That other fella make it?" asked Farmer.

Silke cut her eyes quickly at Elizabeth who was kneeling beside Bear Dog, hugging him.

She shook her head.

Marshal Farmer nodded he understood.

"Believe I'll stay here...ya'll don't mind."

"That's fine, Clay...You did a fine job out there tonight, son, be proud to have you with us anytime...You showed sand."

Marshal Farmer beamed while Clay smiled a little.

"Thank you, sir."

"Be sure to clean and reload your weapon...get in the habit of it."

This time he grinned broadly. "Yessir, Mister Bone."

"And Mister Bone was my daddy…just Bone is fine. Can't stand on ceremony when you've stood shoulder to shoulder being shot at by the bad guys and givin' them tit for tat."

Silke looked at the others. "Ya'll ready?"

Bone grinned. "Waitin' on us you're backin' up."

She wrinkled her brow. "What?"

"Never mind…Lead on, madam."

She strode back toward the causeway. "Not a madam…nor a ma'am."

Bone leaned down to Loraine. "Sounds like Fiona."

"Thinking the same thing."

They covered the two miles to the McPherson cabin in a little over an hour under the light of the full moon.

Bone carried Elizabeth riding on his shoulders most of the way. He lifted her off and set her down at the front door.

She opened it and led the way inside to the well apportioned home.

Padrino found a coal-oil lantern on a table, pulled a lucifer from his vest pocket, lit it, and lowered the chimney back down.

Elizabeth spied her doll on the table in front of the couch.

"Sally," she squealed and hugged the battered rag doll to her chest.

Silke walked into the kitchen, lit another lantern, and then picked up the Arbuckles' can on the counter. As James promised, there was a folded piece of paper underneath. She removed it, unfolded the missive and read it.

"Bone, open the in-ground cooler and look underneath the milk pitchers."

He lifted the two-inch thick, two by two foot cypress plank lid by the recessed ring at one end. The lid was set flush to the floor, and the cooler well was completely underground and stayed cool, even in the summer.

Bone set the milk pitchers and the butter bowl out, reached down to the bottom and removed another plank to reveal a heavy canvas bag at the bottom—he pulled it out.

Loraine stepped over and untied the cord around the top. Inside the bag were bundles and bundles of orange bank notes and several leather bags of gold double eagles.

"Lord, Lord, this is a fortune," mumbled Bone.

"This is what I've been paid by the Pinkerton Agency to find and get back to the KATY…Done my job." Silke hefted one of the sacks of gold in her hand.

Padrino moved over to the counter and grabbed the Arbuckles can. "Bone, if you'll build us a fire, I'll get some coffee on."

"I can do that."

Bone lifted the lid to the cast iron cook stove, grabbed some newspaper, wadded it, and placed it in the bottom of the fire box. Then he picked up several slivers and chunks of pine pitch kindling and laid them on the paper.

"I'd hold up a minute there, Bone."

"What?"

Padrino had removed the lid to the can. He tilted it over a little to show the others what was inside.

"Oh, my gosh." Loraine peered down at the contents that completely filled the can.

Bone looked. "Ho–ly–cow…Fresh water pearls. Blues, wines and whites." He looked at the others.

"There must be fifteen or twenty thousand dollars worth there...Looks like most of them are perfect, too."

Elizabeth ran over to see what the excitement was. "Oh, those are my marbles."

"Marbles?" asked Loraine as she took a large wine pearl from her pouch. "Like this one your cousin gave us?"

"My cousin?"

Silke pointed to a picture on the wall of Maggie. "Yes, Maggie, your cousin gave each one of us a pearl." She took her wine pearl out of her pouch and held it up between her thumb and forefinger.

A puzzled expression came across Elizabeth's face that rapidly turned sad and her lower lip quivered. "Margaret, uh...Maggie died two years ago...Those bad people chased her into the lake...she drowned...She was only sixteen."

Bone, Loraine, Padrino, and Silke exchanged long looks...

§§§

EPILOGUE

HORSE ISLAND

Clay sat on his blanket outside his tent to clean his Peacemaker by firelight. He finished wiping it down with gun oil after he had cleaned the corrosive black powder residue from inside the barrel.

He angled the pistol to the flickering fire, held a piece of white paper, he kept in his kit, between the cylinder and barrel, while he peered down the barrel. Satisfied, he turned the .45 around and inserted five rounds, one at a time, closed the gate, and set the hammer on the empty chamber. Clay twirled it once and dropped it into the holster at his hip.

"Got'ny coffee?"

"Do," replied Marshal Farmer. "Your leg broke?"

Clay grinned, grabbed his tin cup, got to his feet, moseyed over to the fire, picked up the hot pot with his right hand, using one of his folded over deerskin gloves. He set the pot back down, blew across the top of the coffee, licked the rim, and then took a sip.

"Mmm, good coffee."

"Thanks," said Daisy.

"May have to keep you around a while." He smiled.

"Don't get smart." Daisy slapped him across the chest playfully.

Etta's piercing scream shattered the night time soft sounds of frogs and crickets.

Everyone looked at her, and then where she was pointing.

One of the shiners, Cobb, stood at the edge of the firelight, holding his Spencer rifle at his hip, pointing in the direction of the teens and Marshal Farmer.

"He's one of them!" Etta's finger shook. "He did horrid things to Jed."

"Don't none of ya'll move. Everbody just sit down…'cause I'm fixin' to kill the lot of you. Ya'll 'er responsibil fer killin' all my family…You blowed our island to hell an' gone."

Cobb was literally slobbering with the drool running down into his already nasty beard.

"Not gonna happen, you scum suckin' pig."

Cobb swung his rifle to Clay. "Sez you, kid…Yer gonna be first."

"Don't think so."

Cobb's thumb pulled the hammer to the carbine back—it never reached full cock as the tremendous ear piercing sounds of three back to back explosions, rocked the camp.

Three audible thwacks of bullets striking flesh could be heard.

Cobb staggered back with each impact of the .45 caliber slugs from Clay's Colt as he triggered the first and fanned the next two.

The shiner slammed to his back, dead before he hit the ground, the rifle flew from his hands to land behind him in the darkness.

The huge cloud of gunsmoke slowly drifted off into the night as Marshal Farmer and the other teens stood in shocked awe. They looked first at Clay, still holding his gun pointed where the shiner had been standing, then at Cobb on the ground, then back at Clay.

"Told you," he muttered.

"That's from the camp," said Bone as they heard the three rapid shots. "Sounded like a semiautomatic...but they don't have one. Let's move."

He lifted Elizabeth to straddle his neck and broke into a fast jog for the final two hundred yards to the camp. "Hang on girl."

The others followed with Padrino bringing up the rear.

"Ya'll go ahead, I'll be there quick as I can."

He knew he couldn't keep up with the much younger trio.

In less than five minutes they were splashing across the causeway and into camp.

Bone set Elizabeth on the ground as he noticed the last of the gunsmoke drifting out of the area.

"What happened?" He looked around, and then saw the body of the shiner across the clearing. Bone glanced back at Silke and the others. "Must be the shiner James said he saw heading for his place in the pirogue…last of the Mohicans, so to speak."

"Clay took him out while he was holding that rifle on him…Just drew an' fired three shots so fast you couldn't see it," said Marshal Farmer. "An' the guy had Clay covered…Dangdest thing I ever saw…an' he never even spilt his coffee."

Bone nodded. "Called eye to hand delay. The human eye can't get the signal relayed to the hand near as fast as you might think…A good gunman can draw and fire up to four times faster than someone's reaction…but he's got to be cool headed."

"Bone was tellin' me about that when we were on the way over to the shiner's island...Wasn't too sure at the time, but glad I believed him," said Clay. "Didn't figure had anything to lose."

Silke walked over to the body, leaned over and inspected the wounds, and then turned to the others. "I can cover all three holes in his chest with my hand...an' I have a little hand...That's some shootin', Clay."

"Don't let it go to your head though, Bub. Overconfidence is a sure way to get you killed...There's always somebody better."

Clay looked at his father. "I know, Pop...Believe me, I know."

"Need to pack up an' head back to town in the mornin'."

Silke turned to Marshal Farmer. "Also need to tell the local sheriff about those women and children we freed. You know they don't know where to go...They're goin' out into a new world an' will be needing a lot of help."

"I know the sheriff in Jefferson an' he'll know the sheriff of Harrison County, where we are now...You're right Silke, those pore souls will be needin' help."

The following morning at daybreak, they loaded up the pack mule, saddled the horses, crossed the causeway, and headed west toward Jefferson.

Silke took one last look back at the island, and for a moment she saw Maggie standing between Timothy and James watching them leave with Elizabeth—the three were holding hands.

"Bone, look."

He twisted in his saddle and looked back. "What?"

Silke looked again—they were gone. "Oh, nothing." She looked one more time.

JEFFERSON, TEXAS
TEXAS & PACIFIC DEPOT

The entire group, consisting of Silke, holding Elizabeth's hand, Bone, Loraine, Padrino, Marshal Farmer, and the teens located seats in the last passenger car of the north bound train to Denison. They would change trains from the KATY to the Sante Fe west to Gainesville.

"Should get home 'bout two o'clock...all things considered," said Marshal Farmer.

"Sweet Faye will undoubtedly be there to meet us. Told her we would be coming in this afternoon in a telegram," said Padrino.

"Uh-huh," commented Bone as he grinned like a Cheshire cat.

Padrino smiled back and shrugged.

Silke and Bone split carrying the gold coins and the bank notes which they would deliver to the KATY office in Denison. Silke also had put all the pearls into a cloth bag, and then in her saddlebags. The pearls would assure Elizabeth was well taken care of, financially.

"Be glad to get shed of this railroad money. Never comfortable carryin' money that doesn't belong to me," commented Silke to Bone.

"I'm with you there, kid. Not high on my list either.

Bear Dog took his customary place on the floor under Silke's feet. He took a deep breath and let it out in relaxation as the train chugged out of the station on its trek to the north.

GAINESVILLE, TEXAS
SANTA FE DEPOT

The big black 4x4x2 locomotive blew steam out both sides from her boiler as she rolled to a stop at the depot.

Silke and the others disembarked from the car down to the platform. She nodded to Bear Dog.

He immediately ran over to a nearby red oak tree, marked it and scratched the ground beside it with all four feet—then pranced back to Silke, very pleased with himself.

"He's a good boy, yes he is." She scratched him behind his ears, and his top lip curled up showing his front teeth in his smile.

Silke looked up to see Doctor Wellman's nurse, Hilda pushing a tall wickerback wheelchair toward them from the depot. Sitting in the seat was Texas Ranger Riley Boston.

"Riley!" Silke handed her saddlebags to Loraine. "Hold these, please, Loraine. I have to give somebody a hug."

Loraine grinned and took Elizabeth's hand as Silke ran up to Riley and Hilda.

She bent over and hugged Riley around the neck, then released him and planted a long kiss on his waiting lips.

"All right, Miss Justice, that's quite enough." Hilda put her hand on her shoulder. "It's only through Doctor Wellman's weakness and good heart that he let him out of the clinic...but the ranger was pitchin' such a hissy fit when he found out from Faye Skeans ya'll were coming in this afternoon."

Silke leaned back and lovingly caressed the side of Riley's face. "Oh, I'm so glad you came...you hardheaded galoot. But, you should have stayed in bed."

"Uh-uh, no way, no day. Been there long enough with Miz Simon Legree here hoverin' over me night an' day."

"Humpf...You have a cracked skull, Ranger. You're still not out of the woods...That's why you could only come if I came along...So you best mind your Ps an' Qs, mister."

He looked up at Hilda. "I know, I know...But I had to see the woman I love."

"You what?...What did you say?" asked Silke.

He turned back to her. "Said I had to see the woman I love."

"Heard you the first time." She grinned. "Just wanted to hear it again." Silke leaned over and kissed him passionately.

Hilda rolled her eyes.

Riley didn't mind.

§§§§§

PREVIEW

the Next Exciting Novel

from

TIMBER CREEK PRESS

RECIPE for MURDER
by
Ken Farmer & Buck Stienke

CHAPTER ONE

COOKE COUNTY, TEXAS
OCT. 27, 2014

"Told you needed to start earlier...already warmin' up... Deer'll be beddin' down." Jim Bob Owenby pushed a head high branch sticking out from a small chinkapin oak sapling out of the way.

"Hell, practically had to sneak out as it was...You know how Sara is about huntin'...Damn, what's that smell?" Ernie Owenby sniffed the air.

The brothers were almost to their bow stands in Frog Bottom in the heavily wooded Red River valley in the northern part of the county.

Jim Bob also sniffed the crisp morning fall air. "Somethin' dead...Probably a deer somebody gut shot and couldn't find..." He pointed. "Comin' from over there."

They walked over to a copse of dogwood saplings. Ernie kicked some of the new fallen leaves aside, and then jumped back, stumbling, to fall on his rear.

"Oh, Jesus Christ! Jesus Christ amighty!"

"Oh, God!" Jim Bob bent over and upchucked his breakfast as he saw the light brown woman's hand, curled almost into a claw, sticking out from under the leaves.

GAINESVILLE, TEXAS

Corporal Stella Johnson, a drop dead gorgeous blonde police officer, wheeled her black and gold squad car into the Radio Shack retail store in a strip shopping center north of Texas Highway 82. She found a parking spot near the front door, pulled in and turned off the ignition of the older Ford Victoria.

She scanned the area around the store briefly, stepped out and locked the patrol unit before heading into the small shop.

The thirty year old sales clerk looked up as she walked in and removed her dark Ray Bans. Her shoulder length ponytail danced around as she scanned the aisles for the radio controlled cars. He stood a little taller as a smile came to her lips.

"See something you like, Miss?"

"Yeah, think I found the right area...He told me what to look for."

Stella walked past him. His eyes never moved from her—the navy blue duty uniform did absolutely nothing to hide her voluptuous hourglass figure—not even the Sam Brown belt complete with a Sig 226, extra mags, cuffs, Stun Gun, and tactical radio.

"We have a great selection, you know...with Christmas shopping starting in a couple of weeks."

"Some folks wait for seasonal sales...not me." Stella shook her head.

Some of the Remote Control cars were Camaros, others stylized fastbacks resembling Mustangs. There were high-lift pickup trucks and Jeeps, but her eyes spotted a desert camo Hummer about the size of a shoebox.

"Bingo." She picked up the box, quickly read the label and nodded.

When she set the box down on the counter, the clerk grinned.

"Great selection, Ma'am…For your son?"

"Nope. Single…no kids." Stella flashed a dazzling smile. "For a friend."

"Cool…that be all for you?"

"It'll do."

He rang up the sale and glanced at her…name tag. "With tax, total comes to $52.95, Officer Johnson. Cash or credit?"

"Cash. Ya'll still take checks?"

"Of course, but have to see your driver's license…company policy, you know." The clerk slipped the toy into a white plastic bag emblazoned with the company logo.

Stella nodded and chuckled as she fished out her check book from a small black purse. "We get to deal with the dummies who try to hang bad paper...DA takes a dim view of those folks."

"I bet."

She ripped the completed check from the burgundy eel skin checkbook and handed it to him. Her driver's license was inside a plastic pouch affixed to the checkbook cover. She held it up for him to copy the license number next to her address on the check.

"Got it."

She snapped the magnetic cover closed and slipped it securely back into her purse. "I know...everybody's goin' to debit cards...Just old fashioned, I suppose."

He nodded as he dropped the receipt into the bag and handed it to her. "Nothing wrong with being a little old fashioned...Fact, nothing wrong with anythin' at all."

His gaze looked her up and down and came to rest on her golden eyes. He was clearly smitten. Her beauty transfixed him for a moment.

Stella blushed, and then she broke into a sheepish grin. "Thanks, I think." She spun around and headed for the door.

GAINESVILLE POLICE DEPARTMENT
DETECTIVE BONE'S OFFICE

The 6'8" detective handed Stella sixty dollars in twenties. "Here you go, Little Bit. Keep the change...Appreciate the little errand."

"No need...I can never repay you for clearing me of that shooting in CPS."

Bone frowned. "Fool of a DA was a total dipstick for trying to hang that crap on you...Murderin' sumbitch was caught in *flagrante delicto* and then lunged at you. You were in fear for your life...That's the operative phrase, girlfriend. A jury of your peers agreed...Simple as that."

"Never been so scared in all my life. Our Chief was no help and the media..."

Bone held up his hand to stop her. "Vipers and satanists, the lot of 'em. All they want to do is to jack up their stinkin' ratings." He made quote marks in the air. "Cop shoots naked unarmed man...See that all the time." He placed one massive mitt on her slim shoulder. "Say...Aren't you supposed to be on patrol with Newman?"

"Yeah. Told him to coffee up while I ran your little errand. Question…What are you gonna do with that thing?"

"You don't wanna know. Now get your bubble butt outta here." He grinned and pointed at the door. "Scat."

Stella smiled, shook her head and headed out to find her partner. She passed Loraine on her way in.

"Hey, Stella."

"Mornin', Loraine…might not want to go in there."

The attractive Senior Investigator stopped in her tracks. A puzzled look crossed her face. She looked over her shoulder and then back at Bone.

"What are you up to?"

"Nothin'." He took a coonskin cap out of a white plastic bag.

"Playing Davy Crockett?"

Bone arched one eyebrow and gave her one of his enigmatic looks. "Philistine."

He raised the whip antenna on the roof of the Hummer and threaded it through a small slit that he had made in the top of the cap. He carefully, slipped the furry cap over the radio controlled car, leaving the tail hanging out behind.

Bone admired his creation. "Perfect."

Loraine watched him slide the whole thing back into the white bag. "What in blue blazes are you making? A furbie like on Star Trek?"

"Woman...they were called Tribbles...and the answer is no. St. John in his office?"

"No. Our illustrious captain is in the break room, getting some coffee and hovering over the box of donuts."

"Super." Bone grabbed the modified Hummer, headed for the door and turned down the hall.

Loraine was hot on his heels. "You're not?"

"I am." He looked behind him to check the hallway as he stepped into the Captain's office.

Loraine stood outside as Bone knelt down behind the industrial gray steel desk. "Pard, your bread's not real done."

"So I've been told." He grinned broadly as he slipped the fur covered toy out of the bag and set it toward the far back side of the knee well. Bone made sure it was facing the occupant's chair. He got to his feet crumpled the white bag and stuffed it into his tan-colored tactical cargo pants.

"Come on, girl. Let's motor."

He moved quickly past her.

She took longer steps to try and catch up, but at five feet two inches, that was more than a simple stretch in the stride.

She whispered in a low voice, "What is that thing?"

Bone looked over his shoulder and grinned. He held his index finger up to his lips.

He mouthed the words. "You'll find out."

His cryptic answer did little to assuage her growing curiosity.

She followed him back to their desks—set side by side at the back of the Investigations Unit office.

Bone slipped into his oversized executive chair—one he bought on his own dime to handle 285 pounds of solid muscle and match his oversized frame. He settled back into the padded leather and shot a quick glance at his partner.

Bone's smile could be called, *I know something you don't know.*

Loraine eyed him for a second. "You know, you kinda look like Mona Lisa."

Bone chuckled. "That chick has a lot more hair…but I'm much better lookin'."

"And more modest."

He shook his head. "Modesty is not one of my many virtues."

"I know…You gonna tell me what's up?"

"Negative."

"Why not?"

Bone held up two fingers on his left hand. A rather thin exotic bracelet of turquoise stones with alien symbols inset in pure gold links dangled from his wrist. It looked strangely out of place on a really big man.

"Two words…plausible deniability." He arched one eyebrow.

"Men," Loraine huffed slightly and flipped open her laptop and tried to ignore him.

Bone flipped up his laptop cover but pushed it a bit farther away from the usual position on his desk.

Outside in the hallway, a slightly overweight baldheaded black man walked by with a oversized coffee mug in his right hand. Two chocolate glazed donuts and a light blue napkin filled his left hand.   Captain St. John was dressed in tan 511 slacks, and a black polo shirt with a Gainesville Police Department logo embroidered on the left chest. He sported a Glock 22 in 40 S&W caliber in a saddle colored basket weave holster riding in a Texas Ranger style belt.

He didn't even look into Bone's office as he passed.

A smile came to Bone's face as he slid open the bottom drawer on his desk and retrieved a black plastic box with two tiny silver levers on the top.

The brilliant detective began counting down from ten in his head. He set the box on his desk in front of his laptop, and stood up a silver rod that had been laid flush in the back.

Loraine watched as Bone carefully extended the telescoping antenna. The complete scheme of Bone's plan became instantly clear.

Captain St. John set the coffee mug on his desk pad and the two donuts beside it. He licked a smudge of chocolate glaze off his index finger and thumb and took a seat.

Two, one. The silent countdown ended. Bone flipped the two control levers to *drive* and *full throttle* simultaneously.

Down the hall, the captain felt something grabbing at his ankles and making a low growling sound. He reacted instantly by slamming the chair back against the office wall, trying to get away.

"Son of a…"

He drew his Glock as he yanked up the desk to get eyes on the attacking creature.

David St. John wasn't sure what kind of animal it was, but the inactive Marine didn't take time to check. He triple tapped it at close range—the sound of rapid gunfire echoed up and down the halls of the normally placid police station.

St. John was still panting as the desk toppled over, sending his coffee and donuts to the carpet. The noise and motion of the RC car ceased as the scent of acid gunsmoke filled the small office.

Bone slammed the antenna down and glanced at Loraine. "Boogie time."

He picked up the remote control in one hand and grabbed his silverbelly Stetson from the hat rack on the wall with the other and headed for the door.

Loraine sat frozen for a second, stunned by the outcome of the prank.

Bone stopped at the door and looked back. "Comin'?"

She nodded and grabbed her purse.

Moomer stick his head out of the break room. "What's goin' on?"

Bone looked over his shoulder as he passed. "Think the Cap'n was cleaning his sidearm."

"Huh?"

St. John stared at the creature that he had killed. Then he saw the two front wheels of the model Hummer sticking out from under the raccoon fur.

"Damn you, Bone!"

§§§

BLACKSTAR MOUNTAIN by T.C. Miller
BLACKSTAR ENIGMA by T.C. Miller

HISTORICAL FICTION WESTERN
THE NATIONS by Ken Farmer and Buck Stienke
HAUNTED FALLS by Ken Farmer and Buck Stienke
HELL HOLE by Ken Farmer
ACROSS the RED by Ken Farmer and Buck Stienke
BASS and the LADY by Ken Farmer and Buck Stienke
DEVIL'S CANYON by Buck Stienke
LADY LAW by Ken Farmer
BLUE WATER WOMAN by Ken Farmer
FLYNN by Ken Farmer
AURALI RED by Ken Farmer
COLDIRON by Ken Farmer
STEELDUST by Ken Farmer
BONE by Ken Farmer
BONE'S LAW by Ken Farmer
BONE & LORAINE by Ken Farmer
BONE'S GOLD by Ken Farmer
BONE'S ENIGMA by Ken Farmer
SILKE JUSTICE by Ken Farmer
SILKE'S QUEST by Ken Farmer

NO TIME to DIE by Buck Stienke

SY/FY
LEGEND of AURORA by Ken Farmer & Buck Stienke
AURORA: INVASION (Book #6 in the BEF) by Ken Farmer & Buck Stienke

HISTORICAL FICTION ROMANCE
THE TEMPLAR TRILOGY
MYSTERIOUS TEMPLAR by Adriana Girolami
THE CRIMSON AMULET by Adriana Girolami
TEMPLAR'S REDEMPTION by Adriana Girolami

MYSTERY
BONE'S PARADOX by Buck Stienke

Coming Soon

HISTORICAL FICTION WESTERN
McGRATH by T.C. Miller

HISTORICAL FICTION ROMANCE
DAUGHTER of HADES by Adriana Girolami
ZAMINDAR and the LADY by Adriana Girolami

SY/FY
ANTAREAN DILEMMA by T.C. Miller

MYSTERY
RECIPE for MURDER by Ken Farmer & Buck Stienke

Thanks for reading *SILKE JUSTICE* If you enjoyed it, I would really appreciate a review on Amazon. My Author Page is:
 www.amazon.com/Ken-Farmer/e/B0057OT3YI
Email - pagact@yahoo.com

Personally autographed books available at my web site:
Web page: www.KenFarmer-Author.net

TIMBER CREEK PRESS